AMBUSHED!

A twig snapped loudly to the west.

Blade heard it and shifted, his back to Geronimo, his finger on the Commando's trigger. Was it coincidence? Or was someone trying to catch them in a pincer attack?

"I make out three on this side," Geronimo whispered.

A moment later Blade spied four figures darting from tree to tree 30 yards off, drawing the net tighter. "Four over here," he reported.

"How did they know where we were?" Geronimo wondered.

"Doesn't matter," Blade said. "If they charge, waste them."

No sooner did the words clear his mouth than a series of bloodcurdling shrieks rent the night and the phantoms closed in.

D1496008

Other titles in the *Endworld* series:

\# 1: THE FOX RUN
\# 2: THIEF RIVER FALLS RUN
\# 3: TWIN CITIES RUN
\# 4: THE KALISPELL RUN
\# 5: DAKOTA RUN
\# 6: CITADEL RUN
\# 7: ARMAGEDDON RUN
\# 8: DENVER RUN
\# 9: CAPITAL RUN
\#10: NEW YORK RUN
\#11: LIBERTY RUN
\#12: HOUSTON RUN
\#13: ANAHEIM RUN
\#14: SEATTLE RUN
\#15: NEVADA RUN
\#16: MIAMI RUN
\#17: ATLANTA RUN
\#18: MEMPHIS RUN
\#19: CINCINNATI RUN
\#20: DALLAS RUN
\#21: BOSTON RUN
\#22: GREEN BAY RUN
\#23: YELLOWSTONE RUN
\#24: NEW ORLEANS RUN
\#25: SPARTAN RUN
\#26: MADMAN RUN

ENDWORLD

#27: CHICAGO RUN
DAVID ROBBINS

LEISURE BOOKS L NEW YORK CITY

Dedicated to . . .
Judy, Joshua, and Shane.
And **Sheba, J.J., Barney, the blasted goldfish,**
the blooming mosquito-eaters,
and (my favorite) the bloody crayfish.
Sigh. Where's a horse when you need one?

A LEISURE BOOK®

August 1991

Published by

Dorchester Publishing Co., Inc.
276 Fifth Avenue
New York, NY 10001

Printed in the United States of America.

PROLOGUE

"If you want my opinion, Sarge, these patrols are a waste of our time," Corporal Lyle Carson commented while trudging along a secondary road located five miles southwest of Technic City. He squinted up at the bright January sun, glad he was wearing his thermal combat fatigues. Even with the sunshine the temperature hovered only in the twenties. If he didn't have the thermal protection he'd be freezing his butt off after seven hours of patrol duty.

"I didn't ask your opinion, Carson," the sergeant responded stiffly from his position at the head of the six-person column. He glanced over his left shoulder, his weathered features creasing in a frown. "And from now on keep them to yourself."

"Sorry, Sarge," Carson said, and leaned forward to whisper to the dark-haired woman in front of him. "What's eating the sarge today, Lavender?"

"I don't know," the woman replied. "And it's *Private* Lavender to you."

"Boy, what a bunch of grumps," Carson mumbled, adjusting the strap to the Dakon II slung over his left shoulder. He patted the fragmentation rifle affectionately, thankful for its devastating firepower. Who knew what they would run into outside the city? Mutations. Scavengers. Raiders. Monsters. There were endless possibilities. They might even run into *him*.

Soon the patrol came to a junction, and the seasoned sergeant held aloft his right hand, signifying a halt. He moved to the center of the intersection and gazed in each direction.

Carson consulted his watch. "It's two P.M. Four more hours and the sun will be down," he commented softly so the sergeant wouldn't hear.

"Afraid of the dark, are you?" Lavender said sarcastically.

"Of course not," Carson countered. "But they say the Shadow does most of his dirty work after the sun sets."

"Most, but not all," Lavender reminded him.

The sergeant returned. "At ease, people. Take five."

"At last," Carson said, pushing his helmet back on his head and scratching his brow.

Private Lavender removed her helmet, displaying her short, curly red hair, and rubbed the nape of her neck. "I can't wait to get back to the barracks and take a nice, hot shower."

"Care for some company?" Carson asked.

"Dream on, asshole."

The three other soldiers laughed.

"Sergeant Sikes," Carson said to cover his embarrassment, "do you think there's any chance this Shadow character will hit another patrol?"

"The higher-ups wouldn't have squads patrolling outside the perimeter fence if there wasn't," Spikes replied. He extracted a map from a shirt pocket and unfolded it.

"I heard tell the Shadow has killed thirty-seven already," Carson mentioned.

"Then you know more than I do," Sikes said, studying the map. "The top brass isn't about to reveal the exact figure. You've been listening to too much scuttlebutt again."

Lavender chuckled and poked Carson in the arm. "As usual you don't know what the hell you're talking about."

"Oh?" Carson snapped. "Shows how much you know, Ms. Stuck-Up. I happen to be good friends with Jessie Malovich, and I bet you've heard of him."

All the rest now focused on the corporal.

"Malovich was the guy mentioned on the news," one of the men remarked. "The only grunt who survived the Shadow's first attack."

Carson squared his shoulders and nodded, pleased at being the center of attention. Despite his stripes the others, except for the crusty sergeant, tended to look down their noses at him because he was career military and they were young brats who were begrudgingly pulling the two-year stints required of all Technic City citizens. Once they'd put in their time they'd go on to lucrative civilian jobs. "That's right," Carson declared, sticking his thumbs under his web belt.

"You really know him?" Lavender asked.

"I don't make it a habit of lying," Carson said.

Sikes stepped closer. "What did Malovich tell you, Lyle?"

"I went to visit him in the hospital," Carson disclosed, automatically lowering his voice although they were in the middle of the Clear Zone, the ten-mile-wide uninhabited strip bordering Technic City. By executive decree, handed down initially by the very first Minister approximately a century ago, not long after the global Armageddon referred to in the history books as World

War Three, no one was permitted to reside in the Clear Zone. Whenever squatters moved in, an army patrol immediately went out and an officer offered them the opportunity to reside in Technic City. If the squatters refused, they were expeditiously eliminated.

"They let you in?" Lavender inquired skeptically.

"I got there the day after it happened, before the big-wigs clamped a security net around him," Carson explained. "He'd been part of a ten-man unit assigned to escort the Director of Intelligence to a Gypsy camp located twelve miles northwest of the city."

"Why would the Director of Intelligence be visiting a bunch of lousy Gypsies?" wondered one of the men.

"Who knows?" Carson said. "My buddy and the soldiers with him had to wait outside a wagon while the Director went in and shot the breeze with the head Gypsy. The meeting took about an hour, and the Director headed back." Carson paused and let his voice drop even more. "The attack took place just four miles from the west gate."

"Did Malovich actually see the Shadow?" Lavender queried, caught up in the narrative.

"Yes, but not a good look," Carson said. "He told me this big son of a bitch appeared out of nowhere, blocking their path. He asked if they were Technics. The Director informed him they were." He stopped.

"What happened then?" a stocky man asked.

"Yeah, don't keep us in suspense," Lavender added.

Suppressing a grin, Carson said, "The big guy spoke four words and cut loose, mowing them down where they stood."

"What four words?" Sergeant Sikes asked.

"This is for her," Carson quoted.

"Her? Her who?" Lavender asked.

"How the hell should I know?" Carson answered. "I'm

only relaying what Malovich told me. He swore it was the truth.''

For half a minute none of them bothered to speak. At last Sikes cleared his throat.

''Well, even if the bastard is still lurking out here, sooner or later a patrol will nail him.''

The stocky man frowned. ''If this Shadow is so damn dangerous, why don't they send out the Elite Squads instead of common grunts like us? Why use fifty patrols made up of ordinary troopers when the Elite commandos are ten times better?''

''Because there are only ten Elite Squads and they can't be everywhere at once,'' Sikes replied, and touched the radio clipped to his belt above his left hip. ''Why do you think we have this? If we spot anyone suspicious, all we have to do is call in and an Elite Squad will be out here to help us within two minutes.''

''I just hope that's enough time,'' the soldier said.

Sikes folded his map. ''Okay. Enough gabbing. We have a lot of territory to cover before we can head back, so let's get our butts in gear.''

''The sooner we're in Technic City, the better,'' Carson stressed. He watched Lavender replace her helmet, wishing she would be friendlier, longing to have her accept just one of his many advances. She gazed past the sergeant and suddenly froze, her mouth slackening. Puzzled, he looked in the same direction and his breath caught in his throat.

''We go left, people,'' Sikes informed them, and turned, discovering the stranger.

He stood calmly in the middle of the intersection, a huge man with penetrating blue eyes, striking silver hair, and a sweeping silver mustache. A one-piece dark blue garment covered his superbly muscled form. On his left hip rode a survival knife; on his right an unusual curved sword in a leather scabbard. In a shoulder holster under his left arm rode a revolver; in a similar holster under his right nestled an auto pistol. Clutched in his brawny hands was a carbine wth an exceptionally long magazine.

"It can't be!" the stocky soldier blurted out.

"No one make a move," Sergeant Sikes warned in a whisper. "We all have our Dakons slung and he'd cut us down before any of us brought our weapons to bear. Wait for an opening, for my signal."

Carson absently nodded. He couldn't understand where the man in blue had come from. The nearest cover was over a dozen yards away. How had the guy managed to get there without being spotted?

"Hello," Sikes said, much louder than necessary given the fact only 20 feet separated the patrol from the mystery man. "May we help you?"

Without responding, the man in blue came forward ten feet and halted. His eyes seemed to bore into each one of them.

Sikes casually placed his right hand on the sling to his Dakon II. "What do you want? Who are you?"

"You know who I am," the man replied in a low tone.

"Oh, God!" the stocky grunt blurted out, completely overlooking the fact it was illegal for any Technic City citizen to ever refer to any deity.

The man took several more strides. "Place all of your weapons on the ground at your feet and raise your hands over your heads."

"We can't do that," Sergeant Sikes said, inching his hand a bit higher.

"Do it or die."

"There's six of us and only one of you," Sikes blustered, and swallowed hard.

"I know the odds are in my favor," the man said

matter-of-factly. "Your superiors have been grossly negligent in sending out such small patrols."

"We've heard about you, Shadow," Sikes revealed, stalling, his hand sliding higher on the sling.

A lopsided smile curled the big man's lips. "Is that what they're calling me? How appropriate. But by the time I'm done they'll be calling me much worse."

"You're the one who has killed thirty-seven Technics," Sikes noted.

"Fifty-three."

The stocky soldier whined. "Oh, God! Oh, God!"

"Lay down your weapons," the Shadow repeated. "Either comply or use them."

Carson couldn't move. His limbs were locked in place, his mind stuck in neutral. Fear dominated his being, filling every pore, every cell. He knew if he twitched he'd be dead, and he desperately wanted to live.

"Go to hell!" Sikes suddenly barked, and attempted to bring his Dakon into play.

It all happened so incredibly fast. Had Carson blinked he would have missed the fight. He saw the sergeant sweeping the Dakon down and around, but the guy in blue already had the carbine leveled. The automatic burped. Heavy slugs tore into Sikes's torso, and burst out his back to hit the stocky grunt even as the impact propelled Sikes rearward. Both men went down.

Private Lavender had her Dakon only partially off her shoulder when several rounds drilled into her forehead and toppled her on the spot.

The remaining pair of troopers tried to unsling their Dakons, but they each died on their feet, their brains cored in a millisecond of time.

Silence descended.

Feeling his heart thumping wildly in his chest, Corporal

Carson stayed rooted in place. The big man's Carbine swung to cover him and he flinched, expecting to feel searing pain in his chest or head an instant before he plunged into oblivion. Amazingly, no shots were fired. He glanced down at the bodies all around him, marveling at the Shadow's marksmanship. When he glanced up again the man in blue was striding toward him.

"What's your name?"

Taking a deep breath and licking his lips, Carson managed to squeak, "Lyle Carson, sir."

"Do you want to live, Lyle Carson?"

"Yes. Oh, yes."

The big man stopped and studied the corporal's face. "Curious, isn't it, how fear can be a lifesaver given the proper circumstances?"

"What?" Carson mumbled, struggling to get his mind to function.

"Your fear saved your life," the Shadow eleborated, and pointed at the soldier's groin.

Bending his neck, Carson was stunned to find a wide wet stain on the front of his pants, and realized he'd emptied his bladder. How could he do it and not even know it? He looked at the man in blue and mustered a feeble grin. "Sorry."

"Don't apologize to me. I'm not the one who's going to smell like the hind end of a horse until those pants are washed." The Shadow extended his left hand and said, "Now hand over your Dakon or suffer the same fate as your fellows."

Nodding vigorously, Carson complied, bothered by how the guy knew the name of the special weapon used only by the Technic troops. Not many outside of Technic City were familiar with the unique rifle.

The Shadow cast the Dakon aside. "I've spared you for a reason. So long as you cooperate, you'll live."

"I'll cooperate," Carson said quickly. "Anything you want, you get."

"I want answers. Lots and lots of answers."

Carson stared at Lavender, at the ragged hole in the back of her head, at the brains and fluid oozing out of her cranium, and felt a chill ripple down his spine. "Ask away."

"Somehow I knew I could count on you."

CHAPTER ONE

The quaint settlement was located 15 miles northeast of the former town known as Rochester, Minnesota. It consisted of a mere nine buildings that had been constructed from whatever had been handy at the time the buildings went up. To most wanderers passing through it seemed as if a strong, gusty wind would flatten every structure. Optimistically dubbed Second Chance by its grizzled, cantankerous founder several decades ago, the settlement now served as a gathering point for all the farmers, trappers, and others living within 50 miles.

On the Sunday afternoon of the raid there were 65 people in Second Chance. Thirty-one belonged to various families that had traveled in by horse and wagon to hear the bearded man who called himself a preacher discourse on the reality of Heaven and Hell. His late-morning sermon stressed the fact they were all living in a hell spawned by a vile humanity, a hell that surpassed its Biblical counterpart for sheer wickedness and despicable brutality. He urged them to turn to God if they desired to escape the nightmarish legacy bestowed upon them by war-crazed leaders 106 years ago.

The preacher's sermon had concluded two hours before, and the families were strolling about along the dusty main street—if such it could be called—as was the custom in Second Chance on comparable lazy Sunday afternoons. The bartender at Glisson's Shine and Feed was doing a brisk but discreet business as many of the men came in ostensibly to see about purchasing supplies, and quite naturally slaked their thirst while contemplating their expenditures.

Into the town from the north rode the colorful prospector called Old Jerry astride his ancient donkey Jeffrey, waving his arms, his tattered coat flapping, and shrieking at the top of his ancient lungs that they should all flee to the woods. He reined up in front of Glisson's, spilling from his mount rather than taking the time to dismount properly. From all directions hastened everyone in town, aroused by his cries and anxious to determine the cause.

Through the handcrafted batwing doors strode burly Ike Glisson, wiping his hands on his apron and bestowing a baleful glare on the man who had done more than any other living person to keep him in business. "What the hell is all this racket, then? Are you drunk again, Jerry?" he demanded.

"They're comin'! They're comin'!" Old Jerry croaked, rising unsteadily and motioning to the north. "For God's sake, get everyone out of town!"

"Who is coming?" inquired one of the bystanders.

"Raiders," Old Jerry answered. "Dozens of 'em. Saw 'em with my own two peepers."

The news electrified the bystanders. Exclamations of alarm erupted, and mothers scooped their small offspring into their arms.

"Now hold on, folks," Ike called out. "Let's get the facts straight before we get into an uproar." He waited for them to quiet down a bit, then stepped down the wooden steps and towered over the prospector. "Have you been hitting the shine again, old-timer?" he politely inquired, and sniffed loudly.

"I ain't had a drink since sunrise," Old Jerry replied angrily, his eyes blazing resentment.

"Where did you spot these raiders?"

"About two miles north of my shack. I went up the hill behind my place to get me some wood for my stove, and I was sittin' there restin' after doing a bit of choppin'," Old Jerry related. "I happened to look to the north and there they was, a whole bunch of mounted men ridin' toward me."

Ike chewed on his lower lip for a few seconds. "How many riders were there?"

"I stopped countin' at twenty-four."

Another man interjected a question. "How could you tell they were raiders if they were two miles off?"

"I took a gander at 'em through my binoculars," Old Jerry responded. "What do you think I am, stupid?"

No one bothered to give an honest answer.

"Were they armed?" Ike asked.

Jerry snorted. "Do you think I'd be this excited if they was totin' flowers? Of course they had guns, you blamed idiot. Rifles and automatics and the whole shootin' match."

One of the sturdy farmers moved forward. "It must be raiders."

"What are we going to do?" a woman named Linda demanded.

"We don't stand a chance," commented a companion of hers.

A general commotion broke out again. Some of the

youngest children, sensing the panic in many of the adults, provided the proper background chorus for the occasion by crying and whimpering.

"Calm down!" Ike thundered, moving to the top of the steps. "We've got to stay calm and plan on how best to defend Second Chance."

"Second Chance, hell," remarked a devout churchgoer. "We've got to get out of here pronto."

"It's every man for himself," chimed in someone else.

"And don't forget about the women and kids," added a third voice.

The hubbub grew louder as everyone tried to talk at once. Ike shouted for silence, but no one paid him the slightest attention, which only made him shout louder.

Standing next to Jeffrey, Old Jerry broke into a lop-sided grin and shook his head. "Danged fools," he said into the donkey's long ear. "They don't have the sense the good Lord gave a turnip." He surveyed the crowd, and as his gaze strayed to the west end of the street he spied the three men standing silently and observing the proceedings. His first thought was automatic: "That's the biggest son of a bitch I've ever laid eyes on." Then he went up the steps and tugged on Ike's shirt.

"What do you want?" Glisson snapped, still trying to quell the spreading fear.

"Look!" Old Jerry urged, jabbing his finger to the west. "Look at 'em."

Ike glanced around, did a double take, and vented a roar that would have done justice to an elephant-sized mutant. *"Look over there!"*

Most of the crowd swiveled in the right direction, and they all went rigid in their tracks, astounded by the arrival of the newcomers.

The trio walked slowly forward.

"They must be raiders!" a man yelled.

Old Jerry abruptly remembered the many stories he'd
heard while sharing many a meal around many a campfire,
and chuckled. He knew who the one in the middle was,
and he snickered and stated for all to hear, "They ain't
raiders, you nincompoop."

On the right walked a lean man attired in buckskins,
the traditional garb of the postwar era. His shoulder-length
hair and full mustache were both blond, his eyes a lively
shade of blue. A smile played on his lips. Draped around
his waist were two holsters, and in each rode a pearl-
handled .357 Colt Python revolver. Slung over his left
shoulder was a Marlin 45-70. He strolled down the street
projecting an air of nonchalant arrogance, his wide
shoulders swinging with every step.

On the left walked a contrast to the gunfighter. This
man had Indian blood in his veins as evinced in his finely
chiseled features. He was short and stocky, built like a
powerhouse, and dressed in a green shirt and pants, both
sewn together from the remnants of a canvas tent. His
hair and eyes were dark, his face clean-shaven. In his
hands he held an FNC Auto Rifle. In a shoulder holster
under his left arm was an Armanius .357 Magnum.
Tucked under his belt over his left hip was a tomahawk.

While both these men were striking in their own right,
they were dwarfed by the giant in the center, a colossus
seven feet in height and endowed with bulging muscles
that seemed to ripple and flow even when his arms were
at rest. A black leather vest barely covered his chest.
Green fatigue pants and black combat boots completed
his apparel. On each stout hip hung a big Bowie knife.
Bandoleers crisscrossed the vest. And clasped in his left
hand, its stock resting against his side, was a Commando
Arms Carbine.

No one spoke as the trio approached and halted. Ike

walked tentatively down the steps and through the crowd until he stood six feet from the threesome.

Old Jerry stayed abreast of the civic leader.

"Hello," the giant said in a friendly voice.

"What the blazes is all the ruckus?" the gunfighter queried.

Ike addressed them, the words squeaking out unnaturally. "Who are you?"

"We're just passing through," the giant replied. "We don't mean you any harm."

The blond took a step nearer, his hands drifting to within inches of those Colts. "I recollent askin' you a question, friend. It'd be polite of you to answer."

"Hickok?" the Indian said sternly. "Behave yourself."

"Hickok?" Ike repeated, comprehension dawning, and took a step backwards.

An impish grin creased the gunfighter's features and he looked at the Indian. "I'm so famous, it's pitiful."

"Pitiful is the operative word," the man in green commented.

"Keep it up, pard," Hickok growled.

The giant looked from one to the other and they immediately adopted serious expressions. Next he shifted his attention to Ike Glisson. "We couldn't help but overhear. Did someone report raiders in the vicinity?"

"Yes, sir," Ike said, nodding at the prospector.

"I did, Blade," Old Jerry confirmed, proud to be speaking to the most famous man in the Outlands or anywhere else. "Upwards of two dozen of the varmints."

Hickok inexplicably cackled.

"What did you say?" the Indian asked.

Mystified, Old Jerry said, "Upwards to two dozen."

"No, the last word you used," the Indian said.

"Varmints."

Again the gunfighter cackled.

"I don't get it," Old Jerry said. "What's so blamed funny?"

Hickok nearly doubled over with laughter.

"Ignore them," Blade stated, moving closer so he could be heard over the gunman's mirth. "How soon before these raiders get here?"

"At the rate they was movin', I'd guess an hour, tops," Old Jerry said.

"Do you plan to fight?" Blade inquired.

Ike swept his arm towards the onlooking farmers. "What chance would we have against men who kill for the fun of it? We're mostly farmers and simple businessmen. The raiders would mow us down."

"Then what will you do?"

A farmer named Patrick answered. "We'll take our families into the woods and hide out until the bastards are gone. If we're lucky they'll be in a hurry to get elsewhere and they won't burn Second Chance to the ground before they go."

"Wishful thinking," Blade said, his gray eyes sweeping over the crude buildings. He idly brushed at the comma of dark hair hanging over his right eye. "You know as well as I do that most raiding parties have a scorched-earth policy. What they don't steal they destroy."

Hickok stopped laughing and straightened. "Raiders are wimps."

"That's easy for you to say," Ike said.

The giant placed his right hand on his hip and frowned. "We really can't afford any delays, but we can't leave you people in the lurch either. How would you like our help?"

"What can the three of you do against so large a band?" Ike questioned.

"Our best," Blade answered, scanning the crowd, noting the presence of the young boys and girls.

A woman in her twenties moved forward. "My name is Jennifer Shelly. I've heard of you." She paused. "You don't have to risk your lives for us. From what I hear you've all got families of your own."

"Riskin' our skins is what we do best," Hickok said. "Besides, if there's only twenty or thirty of these yahoos, we'll hardly work up a sweat."

"Speak for yourself," the Indian stated.

"Come on, Geronimo," Hickok declared. "We've faced worst odds."

"And we've just managed to pull through by the skin of our teeth," Geronimo mentioned. "I don't know about you, but I like the idea of seeing my wife and son again."

"And I don't?"

Blade turned in a circle, studying Second Chance. "We'll make our stand here. Get all of your people out of town and into the trees."

"Yes, sir," Ike said in transparent relief.

"You can run if you want," Old Jerry said, "but I'm stayin' and helpin' the Warriors."

The giant glanced at him, smiling kindly. "That won't be necessary."

"I'd never be able to live with myself if I turned tail."

"I understand. But you'll be doing us a favor if you go with the rest," Blade said. "If we have to keep an eye on you, the distraction could cost us dearly."

Old Jerry wiped the back of his left hand across his runny nose, his mouth curling downward. "Well, if you put it that way, I reckon I'll skedaddle."

Geronimo, oddly, groaned.

"What's your name?" Hickok inquired, moving up to the prospector.

"Jerry. Folks call me Old Jerry."

"I'm right pleased to meet you," Hickok said. He extended his right hand.

Old Jerry shook, surprised by the controlled strength in the gunman's fingers. "The honor is mine."

The giant hefted his Commando and boomed out instructions. "Okay. You've all heard our decision. Grab whatever food and clothing you want to take and seek shelter in the woods."

"How will we know when it's safe to come back?" a trapper inquired.

Blade's eyes acquired a flinty tint. "You'll know," he told them, and emphasized the declaration solemnly. "You'll know."

CHAPTER
TWO

The Minister of Technic City was *not* in a good mood. He stood on the tenth floor of the Central Core, his hands clasped behind his slender back, scarcely noticing his somber reflection in the tinted window. His shock of hair resembled a handful of soggy straw. His eyes were the hue of a stagnant pool. Both accented his pale complexion and the worry lines etching his face. By contrast, his brightly colored uniform would have been ideal for a performer in one of the prewar circuses. The pants and the shirt were bright, light blue, trimmed in gold fabric. Attached to each of the shirt lapels was a glittering gold insignia; a large T enclosed in a gold ring with a gold lightning bolt slashing through the center.

He gazed out over the metropolis, pondering his problem.

The former city of Chicago throbbed with vitality. Cramming the highways and byways were thousands of three-wheeled motorcycles—trikes, as they were commonly called—and a lesser number of four-wheelers, the only forms of motorized transportation citizens were permitted to own. There were also electric buses, military jeeps and trucks, and a few luxury limousines—one of the perks reserved for the elite in Technic society.

Although the streets were packed with vehicles, the sidewalks were virtually empty, the reason being that a law had been enacted shortly after the holocaust prohibiting citizens from using sidewalks unless they first obtained a written permit. The founders of Technic City, scientists at the Chicago Institute of Advanced Technology who had refused to evacuate during the war and later came to rule the city, decreed such a measure to prevent dissidents from gathering and inciting the rest of the populace into revolt.

The technocrats had done their job well. They'd planned their version of a Utopian society, and had proceeded to rebuild the Windy City from the ground up. Atmospheric Control Stations were erected to provide a constant equitable climate. Grimy factories and towering smokestacks were replaced by streamlined industrial edifices that produced no pollution. Every individual residence had been razed, and the homeowners housed in geometrically designed structures constructed using an impervious synthetic compound invented by the technocrats.

It had been only fitting that the new leaders elected to rename Chicago and christen their creation Technic City. Their brainchild had flourished, the citizenry strictly controlled by the Directors of the various administrative Divisions. The Directors, in turn, were accountable to the Minister. Trade relations were established with other city-states to acquire the few items Technic City couldn't artificially reproduce.

For a century all had gone well.

A scowl reflected the Minister's frame of mind as he

contemplated the consequences of his predecessor's misguided attempt to prematurely seize control of the country once called America. The previous Minister had concocted an elaborate plan that involved penetrating into a special vault located far under the ruins of New York City to obtain huge quantities of mind-control gas stored there since World War Three. Unfortunately, part of the plan had entailed duping the Warriors.

The Minister's scowl deepened. The idiot! His inane predecessor should have known better than to tangle with Blade. The giant's reputation was justifiably deserved, as the Technics had found out to their lasting regret. Not only had the scheme to retrieve the gas been thwarted, but the previous Minister had wound up being terminated by the notorious gunfighter named Hickok.

Then there had been the business in Green Bay six months ago. The Director of the Science Division had set up a top-secret, heavily guarded research station there, and developed a means of controlling mass human behavior through radio waves. Once again the Warriors had intervened, slaying the Director and destroying the facility.

The damn, rotten Warriors.

Were they involved now? the Minister wondered. Given the facts, he tended to doubt their participation. Hit-and-run attacks were hardly their style. Who else, though, possessed the audacity to challenge the awesome might of Technic City? Who else would be so—

A door hissed open on the other side of the Executive Chamber.

Turning, the Minister discovered General Julian Schonfeld, the head of the Technic Armed Forces, walking toward the immense mahogany desk at which the Minister labored most of every day. The Minister took his seat and folded his arms on the top, predicting by the troubled expression on the general's face that the news Schonfeld bore would not be good. "Hello, Julian."

"Sir," Schonfeld responded, halting and giving a snappy salute. "I bring bad news."

"Let me guess. It's happened again."

The general nodded. "Another patrol has been attacked. Five bodies were recovered, but there was no sign of the sixth patrol member, a Corporal Lyle Carson."

"The Shadow again?"

"Yes, sir. Ballistics confirmed the same type of weapon was used, an antiquated firearm called a Wilkinson 'Terry' Carbine. There's no doubt it was the Shadow."

Sagging in his plush chair, the Minister idly rubbed his chin and said, "And am I to understand he took a prisoner this time?"

"It's a possibility. But Carson might have survived the attack and fled into the forest. For all we know a mutation got him."

"I doubt it," the Minister stated. "Only one man has survived an attack to date, and Malovich was extremely lucky. From the evidence I suspect the Shadow deliberately left Malovich alive to inform us about his presence."

"We've sent in three Elite Squads to scour the area. If anyone can find the Shadow, they can, sir."

"They haven't had any success yet," the Minister noted dryly. He drummed the fingers of his left hand on the arm of his chair and bitterly went on, "One man and he ties Technic City in knots. We never know where he'll appear next, which gives him a decided tactical advantage. Trading parties, patrols, you name it, he goes after anyone departing or entering, leaving corpses as his calling card. We can't allow this to go on much longer. Already rumors are spreading among the people."

General Schonfeld smirked. "With all due respect, sir, who cares? Rumors are no threat."

"On the contrary, Julian," the Minister said softly, "the right rumor could spark widespread rebellion. With the Resistance Movement spreading its lies and deceptions to all corners of Technic City, the masses have become uncharacteristically restless. It wouldn't take much to make them rise in revolt against us."

"They know better," Schonfeld declared bluntly. "The military would suppress any such treason."

The Minister swiveled his chair to look out at the metropolis critically. "What chance does a drop of water have of stopping a tidal wave?" he asked, his voice so low as to be inaudible.

"Sir?"

"Nothing. What else do you have to report?"

"The Science Division reports the Cy-Hounds will be ready by the day after tomorrow."

His interest piqued, the Minister looked at the officer. "So soon?"

"The project was given a rush priority, remember? The bioengineers have been working on them for three weeks now."

"Three weeks?" the Minister repeated in disbelief.

"Yes, sir. Time flies, doesn't it? The Shadow first appeared thirty-four days ago, if you'll recall. That's the night he killed the Director of Intelligence."

"Poor Morris."

"A good man, sir. I agree," Schonfeld said, moving closer and lowering his voice. "I thought for certain the Tracking Teams we sent after the son of a bitch would take care of our problem. Those German shepherds and their handlers are top-notch."

"Were, you mean."

"Well, yes, sir. The Shadow did wipe out all three

Teams. Frankly, I'm beginning to suspect the guy might be part mutant.''

The comment brought the Minister out of his chair. ''On what do you base this assumption?''

''The obvious, sir. No *human* is as good as this joker. Consider his tally so far. He's eliminated the three Tracking Teams for a total of six prime dogs and six handlers, plus he's slain fifty-eight of our troopers. No one man could do all that.''

''Blade could.''

General Schonfeld's surprise showed. ''The head of the Warriors? Do you suspect it's him?''

''No, not really.''

''In the long run it doesn't matter. The Cy-Hounds will fix his ass but good.''

''You place a lot of confidence in their performance?''

''I do, sir. I've seen several demonstrations of their capabilities, and there's no stopping them. The technology incorporated into their biochemical forms is staggering. We're talking infrared for night missions, enhanced hearing, computerized scent identification, the whole works. They'll track the Shadow down in no time and put an end to our little problem,'' Schonfield said.

''Let's hope they have more success than their natural counterparts,'' the Minister remarked, turning to the window once more.

''Will that be all, sir?''

''Not quite.''

''Yes?''

''I want your honest opinion, Julian.''

''I've never lied to you.''

''I know. Which is why I'm relying on you to tell me the truth now and not simply tell me what you believe I want to hear, like so many of the lower bureaucratic sycophants do.''

"How can you compare me to them, Marcel?" the general asked, his tone conveying his annoyance.

The Minister turned toward him. "I meant no insult. You know that."

"What is it you want?"

A profoundly thoughtful expression marked the Minister's countenance as he gazed around the ornate chamber. "I want your assessment of the computer projection issued by the socialtechs."

Schonfeld chuckled. "Which one, sir? They issue so damn many. Sometimes I think all those sociologist-types do is sit around on their butts devising farfetched reasons for the latest social trends."

"You know which one I mean."

The general pursed his lips and gazed at the polished tips of his black shoes. "I believe I do, yes. The Freedom Scenario."

"And?"

"Computers make mistakes too. So although our newest and best model has predicted the majority of our citizens will rise in a great revolt and sweep all Technic administrators from power in seventeen-point-two years, I'm inclined to doubt it will ever happen. The masses are sheep, waiting to be led around by the collective hand by those with the wisdom to guide them properly."

"I don't share your cynicism."

"Oh?"

"Except for the Romans of antiquity and a few other long-lost empires, name me one world power that has persisted for more than a few hundred years at most."

Schonfeld's brow knit. "I can't offhand. But again, so what? Empires and world powers have crumpled for a variety of reasons. We won't share a similar fate because we're better than they could ever have hoped to be. Our society is perfect."

"Is it?"

"Most certainly. To think or say otherwise is a legal offense, the highest treason."

"I know," the Minister stated rather sadly. "Well, I was curious about your opinion. Thank you, Julian, for the update."

Saluting again, General Schonfeld did an about-face and briskly departed.

The Minister gazed at the closed door for a full minute before he took his seat and pressed a button on the intercom. "Gracie?"

"Yes, sir," the secretary promptly answered.

"Contact the Bioengineering Depeartment and have them send up a complete disk on their Cy-Hound project."

"Right away, sir."

"And inform the head of the project that I want a personal demonstration tomorrow morning."

"Yes, sir."

"One more thing."

"Yes?"

"Send in Ramis."

"Immediately."

Releasing the button, the Minister leaned to the right and opened the middle drawer of his desk. Inside was the microrecording machine, its tiny spools still turning slowly. He stabbed the off button and removed them.

A knock sounded, and a skinny man wearing a red uniform with silver trim came in. "You requested to see me, Minister?"

"Yes." The ruler of Technic City held aloft the spools. "See what you can do with these."

The skinny man crossed to the desk and took them. "May I ask who it is this time?"

"General Schonfeld, Ramis."

Ramis whistled. "Isn't this dangerous?"

"Are you questioning my judgment?"

"No, sir. Absolutely not."

"Then tend to your work and return the spools and the new version within an hour."

Bowing, Ramis wheeled and hurried off.

A particularly malevolent smile transformed the Minister's face into a mask of sheer evil. He rose and walked to the window, admiring his city, his people, his domain. Soon, he reflected.

Very soon.

CHAPTER
THREE

"What's keepin' the lowlifes?" Hickok wondered testily, his thumbs hooked in his gunbelt. He stood on the porch outside Glisson's Shine and Feed, his shoulders propped against the wall to the right of the batwing doors.

"Do you have an urgent appointment?" Geronimo asked from his seat on the top step. He had the FNC in his lap, and was idly watching a flight of starlings to the south.

"We all do," the gunfighter responded. "We've got to find Bricks-for-Brains before he gets himself in a heap of trouble."

From their left, where Blade leaned on a porch post, came an accurate observation. "He already is in a lot of trouble. He went AWOL."

Hickok glanced at the giant. "Are you fixin' to boot him from the Warriors?"

"It's not up to me and you know it," Blade said. "He'll be judged by a Review Board of his peers. That's the rule. His fate will be in their hands."

"But you could end up sittin' on the Board," Hickok noted. "We all could. How will you vote if you do?"

The giant looked at his friend. "I honestly don't know."

"There will be some who want him thrown off," the gunfighter commented. "I won't be one of them."

Geronimo snickered. "Of course you won't. That's because you went AWOL yourself once."

"I had good reason."

"Sure you did. A wet-nosed kid who worships the grass you walk on went AWOL himself and you had to go rescue him," Geronimo said. "But two wrongs don't make a right."

"Which reminds me," Hickok stated suspiciously. "When I went up before a Review Board, there was a vote to decide whether I'd still be a Warrior or not." He paused. "As I recollect, the vote was two to one in favor of me keepin' my position."

"Yes. So?"

"So there were three Warriors on that board. Rikki-Tikki-Tavi, Carter, and you. One of you crumbs voted no."

"It wasn't me."

"You mean to tell me that you had your chance to get me good and you blew it?"

"Our Triad wouldn't be the same without you," Geronimo said.

"Gee, thanks."

"We'd miss all the humor from your juvenile antics."

Blade laughed heartly, then stretched. He gazed along the street of the deserted settlement, wondering if he'd made the wrong decision. A settlement in the Outlands was hardly under his rightful jurisdiction. Technically, the Home and the Freedom Federation as a whole were his only responsibilities.

Located in extreme northwestern Minnesota, the Home

was a 30-acre compound established by an idealistic survivalist prior to the war. This man, Kurt Carpenter, had become known as the Founder to his followers, those he'd dubbed the Family. Surrounded by a high brick wall and a protective moat, the Home had weathered attacks by scavengers, assasins, and commandos, and even an assault by an invading army.

The Family was just one of seven factions that had formed an alliance called the Freedom Federation. The others were the Free State of California, the Flathead Indians in Montana, the rugged horsemen of the Dakota Territory who had designated themselves the Cavalry, the Moles of north-central Minnesota, refugees from the Twin Cities who'd taken the name of the Clan, and the Civilized Zone in the Midwest and Rocky Mountain region. The Federation was devoted to preserving the flickering ember of civilization in a benighted world.

And here he was, Blade reflected, pledged to defend both his cherished Family and the widespread Federation. As one of the 18 Family members selected to serve as Warriors, he'd taken an oath to safeguard the Family and the compound with his dying breath, if need be. Since his selection as the head Warrior, his duties and responsibilities had multiplied drastically.

With all the work he had to do, what had ever influenced him to also accept the post as the leader of the Federation's elite tactical squad, the Freedom Force? Now he not only had to watch out for the Family, he also had to diligently protect Federation interests wherever he found them challenged or in danger. There could only be one answer, he wryly observed. He was a glutton for punishment.

For added proof all he had to do was take a look around him. Second Chance wasn't part of the Federation; it existed in the vast, wild regions commonly referred to as the Outlands, those existing outside the boundaries of the organized territories. So why in the world was he ready to risk his life yet again for an isolated community, for people he didn't even know?

The answer was simple.

If he'd learned anything during his tenure as head Warrior and with the Force, he'd grown to appreciate the necessity of preventing the hordes of raiders, scavengers, and others from wiping out those devoted souls who were trying to rebuild the world from the ground up. He'd ventured into the Outlands many a time, and on each occasion he'd been fortunate to return to his wife and son alive. But such hard experience had only confirmed his personal conviction that the hordes of darkness weren't going to miraculously go away of their own volition. The legions of death had to be opposed at every turn and gradually eliminated. And he—

"Here they come, pard," Hickok suddenly declared, interrupting the giant's reverie.

Blade straightened and moved down to the street. In the distance swirled a dust cloud, and at its base moved a large group of horsemen. He unslung the Commando and glanced at his companions. "Take your posts."

Geronimo rose and headed toward a two-story building across from Glisson's. "Take care of yourselves," he cautioned.

"Try not to catch any bullets with your noggin," Hickok responded.

"I knew you cared," Geronimo said over his shoulder, smirking impishly.

"I do," Hickok agreed. "I hate to see you walkin' around after a shoot-out with all those dents in your forehead."

"Philistine."

"Same to you," Hickok said, watching the Blackfoot enter the building. He looked at the giant. "What the dickens is a Philistine?"

"Never mind. Take your position," Blade interrupted, moving back up the steps.

"See if I ever ask you a question again," the gunfighter grumbled, walking farther east.

Surveying the interior of the store, Blade discovered a bewildering variety of second- and thirdhand merchandise: torn clothes, slightly dented pots and pans, a variety of farming supplies, steel-jawed traps, axes, knives, rifles, and much more. He peered out and made certain Hickok had entered the fourth structure down, then stood next to the left-hand jamb, where no one outside would be able to spot him, and waited. A tense minute elapsed. Then two.

Finally the pounding of many hooves echoed along the dusty street. Loud whoops sounded, mixed with coarse curses and laughter.

The pots, pans, and other utensils rattled loudly, and Blade had to strain to hear muffled conversation. He pulled the Commando's cocking handle all the way back, and reached behind him to ensure his spare magazines were crammed into his back pockets.

Horses snorted and whinnied as the raiders reined up directly in front of Glisson's. Dust drifted in over and under the batwing doors.

Blade listened to someone laugh, and then a low, raspy voice spoke.

"What a dump. Anyone know the name of this place?"

"Looks like just another armpit to me, Quint," a second man said.

"Doesn't seem to be anyone home," mentioned a third.

"I wonder why," Quint said, sparking general mirth.

"Do we stop for a spell or keep going?" asked the second one.

"I figure we owe ourselves a little R and R," Quint declared. "Let's party till we drop and then burn this dump to the ground."

Blade had overheard enough. He strode boldly through the batwing doors out onto the porch, and suppressed a grin at the astounded reaction of every face turned in his direction. The leading row of horses was abreast of the steps. Halting on the top step, Blade scanned the ragtag collection of motley ruffians comprising the nomadic band and pinpointed the apparent leader, a bearded rider over six and a half feet in height who wore black leather, including a leather patch over his left eye.

"What the hell!" a rider blurted out.

All eyes focused on the Warrior, and not one of them was friendly. He held the Commando at waist height, the barrel slanted downward, his finger on the trigger, and calmly returned their baleful stares.

The leader rode over to within a yard of the steps and scrutinized the giant. "Well, what have we here?"

Blade deliberately said nothing, his gaze sweeping the raiders, counting 32 all told.

"My name is Quint," the leader said. "Who might you be?"

"I'm part of the official Second Chance welcoming committee," Blade replied. "On behalf of the citizens of this settlement, I must ask you to ride on and forget about burning it to the ground."

Quint cocked his head and stroked his beard. "Is that a fact? What if we don't want to ride on?"

"Then every last one of you will die."

Laughter broke out again, nervous laughter, and many of the men nervously hefted their weapons.

"You aim to wipe us out all by your lonesome?" Quint asked.

"No. I wouldn't want to deprive my friends of the target practice," Blade declared loudly.

Geronimo materialized on cue on the balcony of the building across the street. He leaned his FNC on the railing and called out, "It won't be much of a challenge. These yo-yos didn't leave themselves any room to maneuver."

Twisting in the saddle, Quint stared at the Indian. "Just two of you? I don't think we have anything to worry about."

Strolling out a doorway farther down, Hickok smiled at the riders and stated, "I'll take the ten nearest me."

"Three of you?" Quint said, his right hand on his thigh inches from a holster containing an Aminex .45-caliber ACP.

"Three is all it will take," Blade told him. "Do yourselves a favor and ride on out."

"No one tells the Outlaws what to do," Quint snapped, and several of his men fanned out, positioning their horses in a crescent shape around the steps.

"Maybe you've heard of us?" one of them said, and chuckled.

"No," Blade responded.

"I admire a man with balls," Quint said, still maintaining the fiction of politeness. "So here's what I'll do. After we drill you full of lead, I'll see to it that you're given a proper burial instead of leaving your carcass for the vultures and the rotten mutations. I can't be any fairer than that."

"Your generosity is overwhelming."

"I'm serious. Tell me your name and I'll even have the boys carve it into a grave marker."

"The name is Blade."

Quint's sarcastic expression shifted, became immediately concerned. "Who did you say?"

"My name is Blade," the Warrior said, raising his voice for every rider to hear, to give them a taste of their own mocking medicine. "Maybe you've heard of me?"

Silence descended. The Outlaws exchanged surprised looks and fidgeted nervously.

"I've heard tell of a guy called Blade," a grizzled rider mentioned. "They say he always carries two knives—" His voice broke off as he laid eyes on the Bowies.

The leader recovered his composure quickly. He leaned forward, his good eye narrowing. "I've heard of you too. You're the one who licked Crusher Payne and destroyed the Union."

"Payne wasn't the type to listen to reason either," Blade said.

The grizzled Outlaw coughed. "Ain't you the same one who killed the Doktor?"

Blade nodded once. "He made a terrific pincushion."

Whispers spread like wildfire among the band. Everyone in the Outlands was familiar with the tales told about the demise of the most feared man in postwar America, the vile madman who had created an assassin corps composed of genetically engineered hybrids. Merely referring to the infamous Doktor in the presence of children had been enough to provoke nightmares after the children fell asleep.

"What's a man like you doing here?" Quint asked.

"That's my business," the Warrior said flatly.

Quint smacked his lips and folded his hands on his right thigh, letting the reins droop. "There's no reason for you to be so hostile. What have I ever done to you?"

"Not a thing," Blade admitted. "But how many innocent people have you killed during your career? Scores, I bet."

A shrug indicated Quint's dismissal of the subject. "What's it to you?"

"Everything. It's scum like you who are preventing the decent folks of this land from living in peace and attaining prosperity."

At the word "scum" Quint bristled, scowling and stiffening. "No one talks to me like that and lives."

Blade grinned, taunting Quint, and said in complete awareness of the inevitable consequences, "Hot air never scares anyone. You should leave before your big mouth gets you into a situation you're not man enough to handle."

Turning a livid red, the leader of the Outlaws roared his rage and clawed for his gun.

CHAPTER FOUR

Corporal Carson surveyed the confines of the small cave for the umpteenth time and frowned. His gaze drifted to the Shadow, squatting next to a fire near the narrow cave mouth. "How long do you intend to keep me here?"

"Until I'm satisfied," the man in blue responded, shifting to stare at the slope outside.

An involuntary intake of breath came as Carson again laid eyes on the large ebony silhouette of a skull stitched onto the back of the mystery man's one-piece garment. He couldn't imagine why any sane person would want to adorn his clothing with such a bizarre symbol. "Is that outfit you're wearing a uniform of some kind?" he made bold to inquire.

"I'll ask the questions."

"You're the boss," Carson said resentfully. The man never gave an inch. Carson recalled the rapid pace they'd maintained after leaving the site of the attack, and how they'd gone southwest until they were deep in a dense forest. But then he'd lost all track of direction as the big man led him along the base of a series of low hills until they came to one with a cliff on its peak. At the bottom of the cliff had been the cave.

The Shadow turned and sat down, crossed his legs, and folded his hands in his lap. Lying on his left was the carbine. "Tell me about your childhood."

Carson blinked a few times, certain he'd heard incorrectly. "I beg your pardon?"

"Tell me about your childhood."

"You want to know about my life as a kid?"

"Yes."

"Mind telling me why?"

"Yes."

Confused, but not about to antagonize the big man by making an issue of the request, Carson leaned back against the stone wall of the cave and said, "If that's what you want, that's what you get." He paused. "Let me see. Where should I begin? I attended school seven days a week every day of the year until I turned twelve, then I went to work in a factory—"

"One moment," the Shadow interrupted. "Tell me about your parents."

"Okay."

"Your *natural* parents."

Carson's forehead knit as his perplexity increased. "I never knew my natural parents. You must know that all Technic children are taken from their natural fathers and mothers right after birth and given to surrogate parents who then raise them."

The Shadow nodded slowly, his features inscrutable. "I'd heard something to that effect. Explain the reason to me."

"I'm no sociologist. I don't know if I could," Carson said.

"Do your best."

The corporal concealed his annoyance at being asked about such trivial matters, and launched into an explanation. "As best I understand it, the leaders of our glorious city decided decades ago that having kids raised by their natural parents reduced the kids' effectiveness later as productive citizens."

"How?"

"All that emotional crap got in the way. Instead of wanting to be on the job twelve hours a day, those raised by their own folks always wanted time off to be with their relatives and families on days off called holidays."

"So you were raised by surrogates."

"Yep," Carson said. "Great surrogates they were too. Why, they let us spend a half hour with them five days a week."

"How marvelous. And what were you doing the rest of the time?"

"I was either in day-care or school. Compulsory day-care starts at six months of age and continues until three. Then every Technic child is committed to the custody of the school."

"How many hours did you spend at school daily?"

"Twelve."

"The same number you'd later spend on the job."

"Yeah. So?"

"Did you eat your meals at school?"

"Of course. All food was furnished by the government."

"Then you only went home to sleep, basically?"

"More or less," Carson conceded, and grinned. "But we did get to see our surrogates like I told you."

The man in blue bowed his head and sighed. "What an atrocity," he said softly.

"What are you talking about? Everyone in Technic City loves the way things are."

With surprising suddenness the Shadow's head snapped up. "I was told differently. Several friends of mine encountered one of your illustrious Directors in Green Bay, and he revealed that a resistance movement has sprung up."

Carson stiffened. He'd heard about the Director of the Science Division, and the rumor that Darmobray had gone to Green Bay, Wisconsin, to conduct highly classified experiments and been slain by several Warriors.

The Warriors!

"You're one of them!" Carson blurted out, stabbing a finger at the Shadow.

"One of whom?"

Carson took a step forward, insight flushing his countenance with excitement. "You're one of the Warriors, aren't you?"

"Yes."

"What's your real name?"

The man in blue stood, slinging the carbine over his left shoulder as he did. "I chose the name Yama."

"Yama?" Carson repeated. "Never heard of you. I did hear tell about Blade and that gunman, Hickok. Are they here with you?"

"Aren't you forgetting something?" Yama rejoined.

"Like what?"

"*I* ask the questions."

The hard-edged declaration caused Carson to wince as if struck and to move back against the wall. "Hey, I didn't mean to pry. I was just curious, is all."

"And you know what curiosity did to the cat."

Carson nodded and gulped, terrified by the unexpected fire in the big man's visage. Be very careful, he chided himself, or he'll snap you in half like a fragile twig. Carson wished he could escape and get word to his superiors. They'd undoubtedly bestow extra food and entertainment credits on anyone who could confirm the presence of a Warrior in the vicinity of Technic City. Those extra credits would enable him to buy real food for a change, a hamburger even or a hot dog, anything instead of the usual army diet of fried worms and baked beans.

Yama clasped his hands behind his back and gazed out the entrance into the distance. "I suppose I shouldn't hold your curiosity against you. Without a sense of inquisitiveness, humankind would never have established a base on the moon, never have journeyed to Mars. Curiosity stimulates us to momentous achievements."

"Whatever you say," Carson concurred.

The Warrior glanced at the soldier. "Have you ever been curious about what lies beyond the veil?"

"Where?"

"On the other side of this life. Haven't you ever wanted to learn what happens to you when you die?"

"I already know," Carson said smugly. "We're taught in school that this is the only life we get. Once it's over, that's all she wrote."

"Your teachers were mistaken."

"How do you know?" Carson responded sarcastically, peeved at having the Technic educational establishment insulted. "Have you died?"

"Yes," Yama stated.

"What?"

"I died two years ago in Seattle."

"Yeah. Right. And I'm talking to your ghost."

Yama looked at the Technic and grinned. "I experienced an NDE and then returned to my injured body."

Totally confounded, Carson decided to play along until an opening came along for him to make a break. "I'll bite. What's an NDE?"

"A Near-Death Experience. My soul ascended to the

next level, where I saw an amazing edifice and spoke to my Spirit Guide,'' Yama related reverently.

"Sure you did," Carson said, afraid he'd burst out laughing. This guy was a total psycho, and should be locked in a padded room for the rest of his life. "Uh, why are you telling me all of this?"

"So you can explain to your Minister the reason I've come to destroy Technic City."

"All by your lonesome?" Carson queried, and snickered. Then it hit him. The Warrior intended to turn him loose!

"I couldn't very well have asked my friends to assist me," Yama disclosed. "Few of them would comprehend my motivation, and most of them have families. This is something I must do myself, something I should have done four years ago."

"I don't follow you."

"It doesn't matter," Yama said, and walked over to the trooper. "What does matter is that you relay my message to the new Minister. Inform him that unless he agrees to relinquish power to the Resistance Movement, I will topple him from power myself. The Technic system is an abomination that has endured for far too long. Millions of people are being held in social bondage in the name of a perverted science. Technology isn't the be-all and end-all of existence, and shouldn't be used to suppress personal freedom."

Carson felt uncomfortable having the big man's blue eyes locked on his own. He fidgeted and said, "You really expect me to tell the Minister all that?"

"Do your best."

Why should I? Carson said to himself, too scared to voice the thought aloud.

"Because I'm sparing your life," Yama said.

Shocked, Carson recoiled and exclaimed, "How did

you know what I was thinking? Are you a mind reader?''

Instead of answering, Yama stepped to one side and indicated the cave entrance. ''You can leave now. There are still enough hours of daylight left to enable you to reach Technic City if you hurry. Simply head northeast.''

''I can really go?'' Carson inquired anxiously, suspecting a trick. The guy probably planned to shoot him in the back the minute he stepped outside.

''Yes. You've related all I need to know.''

Slowly, tentatively, Corporal Carson moved toward the opening. He disliked the idea of fleeing across the mutation-infested countryside, but he didn't see where he had any choice. If the wacko was going to let him go, then he'd damn well go. In a way he almost felt sorry for the jerk. The guy was 50 cards shy of a deck and not responsible for his actions.

''One more thing,'' Yama stated.

Dreading that he'd been duped, Carson looked at the man in blue. ''What?''

''Be sure to let your superiors know I'm doing this for her, for Lieutenant Alicia Farrow.''

''Who the hell is she?''

''She was a Technic.''

Carson wanted to learn more, but he opted not to press his luck. ''All right. I'll tell them. Anything else?''

''No. May the Spirit watch over you on the return trip.''

''Yeah. No doubt.'' Carson stepped to the cave mouth, paused to glance over his shoulder at the pathetic madman, then dashed down the rock-strewn slope, heedless of the risk entailed. He needed to put distance, lots of sweet distance, between the crazy man and himself. By his estimation these hills were situated at the border of the Clear Zone; once there he might bump into a patrol, and wouldn't have to run all the way to the city.

He couldn't quite believe his good fortune. He was the

only person to ever survive an attack by the Shadow unscathed. The media types would probably be all over him once he returned. Maybe he'd appear on a talk show or two. Hell, within 24 hours he'd probably be the most famous man in Technic City.

Corporal Carson smiled, pleased by his imminent fame. Being captured by the Shadow might well wind up as being the best thing that ever happened to him!

CHAPTER
FIVE

Blade crouched, leveling the Commando, and unleashed a withering burst at a range of eight feet, sweeping the barrel from right to left.

In the act of drawing the Arminex, Quint took a half-dozen slugs full in the chest. The sledgehammer impact lifted him out of the saddle and hurled him over his mount's rump to crash down in the dusty street.

Other nearby riders toppled, their horses neighing and shying at the metallic bleating of the submachine gun.

From the balcony Geronimo opened up, spraying a rain of lead from his FNC. He killed six men in half as many seconds, then ducked as some of the Outlaws returned fire.

At the initial retort of the Commando someone else had galvanized into action. Hickok's arms were blurs as both Pythons leaped from their holsters and he thumbed both hammers with ambidextrous precision. He moved toward Glisson's firing on the run, always going for the head and always hitting the rider he aimed at.

Bedlam ensued in the street as the desperate Outlaws

vainly endeavored to shoot back while keeping their frightened animals under control. Packed together as they were, they were unable to bring their weapons to bear effectively.

Blade darted to the right as rounds narrowly missed him and thudded into the front of the store. He saw a pair of scraggly raiders break from the pack and gallop toward him, one aiming a pistol, the other a Winchester. Throwing himself farther to the right, he rolled to the very edge of the porch and swept to his knees, the Commando's stock tucked against his side.

The rider with the pistol squeezed off a hasty shot.

A breeze seemed to stir Blade's hair, and then his finger tightened on the trigger, the Commando bucking and belching lead.

As if hit by a gigantic invisible fist, the raider was catapulted backwards, and sprawled in a heap in the dust.

The second man had his Winchester leveled.

With a mere flick of his wrist Blade brought the Commando to bear, watching in grim satisfaction as a half-dozen holes blossomed on the man's face and the Outlaw went limp and fell from the saddle. Blade shifted, taking in the melee in a glance, and fired discriminately, making every shot count.

Across the way Geronimo was in trouble. Seven of the riders were pouring a blistering swarm of lead hornets into the balcony, sending wood chips flying from the balcony. The Indian was down low and acquitting himself as best he could.

Blade dived from the porch, flattening and slaying a trio of raiders who broke from the cluster and came straight at him. There were still plenty of rounds left in the special 90-shot magazine the Family Gunsmiths had fitted the Commando with, and he shoved to his feet, staying in a crouch, intending to go to Geronimo's aid. Out of the corner of his left eye he registered a streak of buckskin and glanced around.

Hickok had darted out from behind a post, apparently having just reloaded because he was snapping both loading gates shut even as he appeared. He raced into the thick of the band, spinning and weaving, firing first one Colt, then the other, leaving a trail of bodies in his wake as he sped to his friend's assistance.

The seven killers were concentrating their firepower on Geronimo. They had their backs to the middle of the street, and so had no idea they were in danger until three of them were drilled from behind.

Blade saw two mounted raiders trying to get a bead on the gunfighter. He snapped the stock to his right shoulder, sighted, and bored holes through their abdomens, dropping both.

The quartet of Outlaws still striving to nail Geronimo realized they were being attacked from the rear and spun.

Hickok killed two in the blink of an eye.

Up popped Geronimo, the FNC steady, to blister the last pair.

Blade moved into the street, firing right and left, taking out rider after rider. A stinging sensation lanced his left shoulder, but he ignored the discomfort.

Six of the Outlaws had wheeled their mounts and were in full flight to the east. They looked over their shoulders in terror, as if demons were on their trail.

Stitching a hefty raider in the act of pointing a sawed-off shotgun with holes from the guy's sternum to his crotch, Blade swung toward the center of the street, ready to slay more. It took a second for his mind to acknowledge there were no Outlaws left to fight.

Dozens of bodies littered the dusty ground, and most

in spreading pools of blood. Many were groaning and twitching. There were also nine horses lying on their sides, a few wheezing or whinnying pitiably.

The relative silence after the gunfire was eerie. Blade scrutinized the fallen Outlaws carefully, seeking any who might have a spark of defiance still in them. He saw none, and hastily removed the almost-spent magazine and replaced it with a fresh one.

Hickok stood two thirds of the way to the opposite building, his arms at waist height, his narrowed eyes roving over the Outlaws. He looked at the giant and grinned. "Just like I figured. A bunch of wimps."

Blade walked forward, alert for treachery. There was always the possibility one of the Outlaws might be faking and waiting for the chance to fire.

In another few seconds Geronimo ran from the two-story building and halted, breathing deeply, a thin red line marking his left cheek. "We did it," he said in astonishment.

"Was there ever any doubt we would?" Hickok asked arrogantly.

"Thanks for your help," Geronimo said.

"What help? I like shootin' cow chips in the back, is all."

Halting, Blade frowned at the sight of a horse sporting a nasty, ragged hole in its neck. Reddish spittle flecked its mouth. "Hickok, finish off the Outlaws. I don't want one alive."

"You got it, Big Guy."

"Geronimo," Blade went on, "the horses are yours."

"I hate killing horses."

"Join the club," Blade said. He walked to Glisson's and climbed the steps. A twinge in his shoulder reminded him of his wound, and he tilted his neck to find a shallow crease. Nothing to get upset about. A glance eastward showed the half-dozen Outlaws a quarter of a mile distant and continuing their pell-mell flight. Too bad, he reflected. It would have been nice to bag all of them.

A revolver cracked. Hickok had shot an injured raider at point-blank range. He went from body to body, and those killers he found alive he promptly terminated.

Scowling in revulsion, Geronimo did likewise with the horses. He patted each animal and whispered in its ear before he shot it.

Blade let his muscles and nerves relax a bit. How unfortunate, he mused, that they hadn't been able to bring the SEAL on this trip. Confronting the Outlaws would have been much easier.

The Solar Energized Amphibious or Land Recreational Vehicle had been the brainchild of the Family's Founder. Carpenter had spent millions to have the amazing prototype developed by financially strapped and therefore eager automotive executives in Detroit. Solar-powered, designed to negotiate any terrain, the SEAL was unlike any vehicle that had ever existed or ever would.

Once the engineers completed their task, Carpenter had turned to different experts, mercenaries, who'd outfitted the enormous bullet-proof van with more armaments than a tank. The Warriors had taken the SEAL on many a run to various sections of the country, and it had saved their lives on many an occasion.

But not this time, Blade reflected wryly. Two months ago, while conducting routine maintenance after a trip to the city-state known as Sparta, he'd discovered a crack in the lead-lined case underneath the SEAL that contained the revolutionary batteries used to power the vehicle.

Plato, the Family's Leader, had decided to call in specialists from the Civilized Zone, mechanics who knew the basics of automotive construction and could assist in repairs. When Blade and his companions had departed the

Home, those same mechanics, with the help of selected Family craftsmen, were in the process of welding the case and going over every square inch of the SEAL to be certain there were no other cracks.

Waiting until the van was fully restored would have made the trip less difficult, but the giant had decided he couldn't afford another two weeks of delay. So off they'd gone.

And here we are, Blade noted, scanning the carnage, aiding complete strangers when the three of us should be hot on Yama's trail. He heard muffled voices, and gazed to the west.

A majority of the townspeople, farmers, and trappers were nearing the settlement warily. At the forefront were Glisson and Old Jerry, leading his donkey.

Blade leaned on a post and thought about the irony of the situation. If not for Yama going AWOL, the three of them wouldn't have been anywhere near Second Chance and the Outlaws would have razed it. Truly, as Plato often claimed, the workings of the Spirit were too mysterious to fathom.

Geronimo completed his mercy killings, and began helping Hickok to put the remaining raiders out of their misery.

The crowd hurried toward the Warriors, their fears dispelled when they fully realized the Outlaws had indeed been defeated.

Ike Glisson was first on the scene, his anxious gaze on his store. He noted the bullet holes with disapproval, but mustered a smile and declared, "You saved our town! We can never thank you enough!"

"Is that a fact?" Hickok asked bitterly, and planted a slug in the head of the last groaning raider. He promptly started to reload.

More of the people arrived, their shocked expressions

betraying their true reactions to the slaughter. Mothers turned their children away from the blasted, blood-spattered corpses.

Old Jerry came up to the steps and grinned at the giant. "You're everything they say you are." He nodded at the battleground. "I ain't never seen the like."

"We get a lot of practice," Blade commented.

"So I hear."

"How can we ever repay you?" Glisson inquired, walking onto the porch.

"With information," Blade said.

"Is that all?" Glisson asked in surprise. "We'll help if we can. What do you want to know?"

"We're trying to find a friend of ours. We have reason to believe he's on his way to Technic City," Blade said.

"What's that?" called a man in the crowd.

"Technic City was once called Chicago."

"Never heard of it," volunteered a trapper.

"Chicago was a major American city located in Illinois on the southwest shore of Lake Michigan," Blade patiently elaborated. Their profound ignorance reminded him once again of the deplorable conditions existing in the Outlands. Few could read; fewer still could write. Public education, the proud cultural hallmark of the prewar nations, was no more than a historical footnote.

"What's an Illinois?" someone wanted to know.

Hickok and Geronimo strolled over. The gunfighter twirled his Pythons into their holsters and fixed a critical stare on the assembled Outlanders. "My pard is tryin' to find out something. The next one of you who butts in is liable to get me real riled, if you get my drift."

Scores of lips were suddenly tightly sealed.

Blade smiled and looked at Glisson. "As I was saying, we're after a friend of ours. If he made a beeline for

Technic City from our Home, then he might have passed through Second Chance.''

"A lot of wanderers pass through," Glisson noted. "What does this guy look like?"

"You'd remember him if you saw him. He's almost as big as I am and carries an arsenal. He also wears a dark blue outfit with a black skull on the back."

"Him!" Glisson exclaimed, and many in the crowd murmured.

The three Warriors exchanged excited glances.

"He was here, then?" Blade asked.

"Sure as hell was," Glisson confirmed. "No one in Second Chance is likely to forget him."

"Why not?"

Old Jerry supplied the answer. "Your friend killed three men right there in Ike's place."

Blade's features clouded. "Tell me about it."

The proprietor of Second Chance's leading establishment glared at the grizzled prospector, then provided the details. "Well, a guy wearing the clothes you describe walked into my joint one night well after sunset. I was behind the bar and I noticed him right away. I mean, a big son of a bitch like that stands right out in a crowded room."

"Go on."

"He came up to me and asked for a glass of water. I sort of laughed and asked if he didn't want a stronger drink, but he looked me in the eyes and shook his head." Glisson couldn't repress a slight shudder. "I don't mean no offense or nothing, but there's something about that guy, about his eyes, that can scare the living daylights out of you. Staring into them is like staring into . . . into . . . into living death, if that makes any sense."

"No offense taken," Blade said softly.

Geronimo nodded. "We know what you mean."

"Anyway," Ike went on, "I gave him what he wanted.

It struck me as odd that he'd just waltzed into town. There aren't too many men who will travel the Outlands at night, not with all the mutations and wild animals lurking everywhere, just waiting to rip a person to shreds. Most folks who are on the road and who don't reach a settlement by nightfall generally make a roaring fire and stay up most of the night tending it.''

"We know,'' Blade said, wishing the man would get to Yama.

"So there I was, standing right across from your friend and not knowing what to say or do. The whole room had gone silent when he entered. Everyone sensed that he was a tough one and no one bothered to be friendly.''

"Get to the killin' part, idiot,'' Hickok snapped.

"Yes, sir. The guy in blue had been there not more than a minute when three drunks walked over to him and started making fun of him.''

"Three drunks?'' Blade repeated.

"Yeah. They weren't regulars. Just drifters. They arrived in Second Chance about an hour before sunset and took a room at Mabel's boardinghouse. Later they came in my place and paid for a bottle of shine. By the time your friend showed up they were pretty well soused.''

"What did our friend do?'' Blade inquired.

"He ignored them at first. They were teasing him about his outfit, about the skull on his back. Me and several others tried to get them to leave him alone, but they told us to get screwed. Your buddy finished his water and turned to leave. That's when it happened.''

Hickok made a hissing sound. "If you don't get to the killin' part right quick, there's going to be another killin'.''

Glisson continued rapidly. "One of the drunks asked your friend if his girlfriend knew he walked around dressed like a sissy.''

"Uh-oh,'' Geronimo said.

"Your buddy didn't say a word, didn't even move, but everyone else could tell there was something different about him. I don't quite know how to describe it," Glisson stated. "He seemed to change, to become harder or colder or I don't know what. I never saw anything like it."

"We know what you mean," Blade told him.

"It was spooky. Anyway, he advised the drunks to mind their own business or prepare to embrace eternity," Glisson said, and chuckled. "Those were his exact words. 'Prepare to embrace eternity.' The drunks laughed, of course, and one of them shoved your friend, and they all spoke up and claimed they were going to teach him some manners and give him a bath in a horse trough. He brushed right past them and headed for the door."

"And? And?" Hickok prodded.

"And the dumb-ass drifters went for their guns. I was right behind them so I ducked down low. Half the time in a shootout innocent bystanders also get hit by wild shots. I knew from experience not to be in the line of fire when gunplay erupts."

Hickok came up the steps in two bounds and stood directly in front of the startled business owner, his eyes flashing. "How would you like to see some gunplay right here on your porch?"

"There's not much left to tell," Glisson assured him. "I heard three shots, that was all, and when I peeked over the bar the three drifters were dead on the floor and your friend was going out the door. That's it."

"You mean you didn't actually *see* the killin'?" Hickok demanded.

"No, not exactly," Glisson confessed. "But I heard the shots," he emphasized.

The gunfighter looked as if he wanted to punch someone. Anyone.

"I saw what happened," Old Jerry stated. "I was sittin'

at a corner table nursin' a glass of prime shine and watched the whole blamed thing." He paused. "Never saw anyone as fast as your friend. He had some kind of fancy carbine over his left arm, but he didn't go for that."

"A Wilkinson 'Terry' Carbine," Blade said. "It's one of his favorite weapons."

"Whatever. He also had a couple of guns in shoulder holsters, a pistol and a revolver, if I recollect rightly. When the drifters grabbed for their irons, the big guy in blue went for his pistol. Not one of those jerks even cleared leather," Old Jerry related. "They were downright pitiful."

"You sure have a way with words, old-timer," Hickok remarked.

Geronimo snickered. "You would think so."

"And our friend never said a word after he shot the drifters?" Blade asked.

"No," Glisson said. "He just left. And I can tell you it was at least fifteen minutes before anyone had the nerve to poke their head outside. By then he was long gone."

Old Jerry stared at the giant Warrior. "Do you mind lettin' us know the name of your friend?"

"Yama," Blade revealed.

"Never knew anyone called that before," the prospector noted.

"He named himself after the Hindu King of the Dead," Blade explained.

"He named himself?"

"It's a custom our Family has."

"A king of the dead, you say?" Old Jerry said, and nodded. "Well, it sure as hell fits him. That friend of yours is living death."

Hickok rested his hands on his Colts and sighed. "We know, old-timer. Believe me, we know."

CHAPTER
SIX

Yama moved to the mouth of the cave and watched the Technic soldier descend the slope and enter the forest below. He waited a few minutes, giving the trooper enough time to cover a couple of hundred yards, then hastened out, certain the trees obscured the cave and the slope from Carson's sight. In lithe bounds he ran to the bottom of the hill and plunged into the dense undergrowth.

So far, so good, the Warrior noted, unslinging the Wilkinson as he glided silently in pursuit of his quarry. The second phase of his plan was about to begin.

Had it really been six weeks ago when he'd arrived at the area? The time had flown by, perhaps because he'd spent every waking moment hunting down Technics. His personal war against the technocrats entailed hitting them fast and hard again and again and again.

Of course, he hadn't launched his attrition campaign right away. It had taken him a week or so to scout the territory and locate a suitable refuge. He never would have found the cave if not for his urge to climb that hill so he could survey the countryside and memorize prominent landmarks. The bear den was invisible from the air, with a spring not a quarter of a mile off and ample game in the woods, and its chance discovery had proven immensely beneficial. It was mildly regrettable that the bear had objected to sharing the shelter, but those bear steaks had been delicious and nutritious.

Yama heard the cracking of twigs ahead and slowed. He soon spotted the soldier awkwardly plowing through dense brush in a general northeasterly direction. The fool was making enough noise to attract every beast and mutant within a mile. Yama hoped none would show up in search of their supper, or his entire scheme would be blown and he'd have to capture another trooper.

He trailed the bumbling corporal at a discreet distance, his extensive Warrior training and experience enabling him to move as silently as a panther. The man looked back repeatedly, fear on his features, but never realized he was being followed.

The sun arced slowly across the blue vault of sky toward the western horizon. A cool breeze from the northwest occasionally rustled the leaves. Birds sang and flew about in the treetops.

Yama wished the soldier would go faster. The timing was critical. If the fool wasn't out of the forest by nightfall, it could ruin everything. He detected motion to his left, and pivoted to see a buck bounding away. Carson, naturally, hadn't noticed.

The minutes became an hour. An hour and a half. Finally the corporal burst from the forest onto a road. He cried out in relief, sank to his knees, and kissed the asphalt.

The Warrior concealed himself behind a tree and watched the soldier rise and jog off. Keeping low, he paced the Technic, staying a dozen yards to the rear, using every available cover. Perhaps his ploy would succeed after all. The key lay in finding suitable clothing. Few men were his size. But he would be unable to penetrate to the heart of Technic City without a disguise of some kind.

Corporal Carson had traveled almost a mile when four figures appeared ahead. He halted, apparently undecided whether he should hail them or bolt, until he recognized the uniforms worn by the quartet. Up went his arms and he screeched at the top of his lungs. "Here! Over here!"

The squad immediately raced toward him.

Yama drew up at the base of a thicket, lay flat, and listened.

"Help! Help me!" Carson shouted, breathing heavily, evidently on his last legs.

Advancing four abreast, the quartet closed in swiftly.

"Am I ever glad to see you!" Carson informed them when they were only ten yards away. He bent at the waist and put his hands on his knees, showing every sign of being ready to keel over from his ordeal.

"Are you Corporal Carson?" demanded a man sporting six stripes as the squad drew to a halt.

"Yes, sir," Carson verified. "Serial number TA118757403."

"I'm Sergeant Zeigler," the noncom stated. "There are patrols out all over this quadrant searching for you. We were told the Shadow might have captured you."

"He did," Carson said. "The son of a bitch jumped the patrol I was with. He snuck up on me from behind and knocked me out. When I came around all my buddies were dead. Then he tied my wrists and dragged me off to his cave."

Yama had to admire the corporal's vivid imagination, however much it clashed with reality.

"Where is the Shadow now?" Sergeant Zeigler asked.

"Probably still back at the cave," Carson said. "He'd tied my ankles too when we got there, but later he made the mistake of going out for water. I was able to slip free of the ropes and haul ass. Since he had all the weapons there wasn't much else I could do."

"Why did he take you prisoner and not kill you like all the rest?" Zeigler inquired.

"How the hell should I know?" Carson stated. He straightened and added in a low voice, "I did learn critical information our superiors will be grateful to hear. How soon can you get me to the city?"

"We'll leave immediately."

"Good. But please go slow. I've been running for six or seven miles."

The noncom studied the corporal. "I'm impressed. No one has gotten the better of the Shadow before. You must be a tough one. Have you ever given any thought to joining the Elite Squad?"

"Never figured I was good enough," Carson said humbly.

"Think about it. I can put in a good word for you with my captain and he can get the ball rolling." Zeigler indicated his companions. "We're Elite Squad-A9 by the way."

Yama stayed motionless as the five Technics headed out. Not until they were a few dozen yards off did he rise and prowl along in their wake. The sergeant and Carson were conversing, the rest listening intently, as they hurried toward the city. None paid much attention to the forest.

For all the Technics' vaunted scientific achievements, their soldiers were less professional than others Yama had encountered. He chalked their deficiency up to an over-reliance on technology; they tended to depend on their hardware, and neglected to hone their personal combat skills as fully as wisdom would dictate.

The thought brought a grin to his lips.

Considering his own passion for utilizing a wide range of weapons, he was a fine one to criticize the Technics. In addition to a Wilkinson "Terry" Carbine that had been converted to full automatic by the Family Gunsmiths and fitted with a special 50-shot magazine, he carried a Browning Hi-Power 9-millimeter automatic pistol in a shoulder holster under his right arm, and a Smith and Wesson Model 586 Distinguished Combat Magnum under his left. A 15-inch survival knife on his right hip had often come in handy, but his favorite edged weapon was the curved scimitar resting on his opposite side. His extra long pockets, both front and back, were crammed with spare clips and ammo.

Yama slowed when the Technics reached an intersection and took a left. Pausing until they were out of sight, he quickly crossed the road and resumed stalking them. Every now and then one would look back, but they obviously didn't entertain the slightest suspicion they were being shadowed.

Twenty minutes later the unforeseen transpired. Sergeant Zeigler's squad met another. An excited exchange took place, and the units combined forces to escort the corporal onward.

The Warrior had hoped the troopers would continue all the way to the high fence that completely encircled the metropolis, but a half mile from it they rounded a curve, and strung out before them were four green convoy trucks and five jeeps parked along the right side of the road, plus scores of soldiers involved in various activities.

Now Yama had to be extremely cautious. More troopers increased the likelihood that one might glance into the woods and accidentally spot him. He bent at the waist and slowly neared the vehicles.

Carson's arrival created quite a stir. Practically all the

soldiers converged on him. He was clapped on the back and heartily congratulated. A pair of officers took charge and ordered the troops back to work, then walked with the corporal to a jeep.

The Warrior's calculated scheme hovered on the brink of disaster. He'd intended to use the distraction of Carson's arrival at one of the perimeter gates as his ticket to gaining entry to Technic City, but he couldn't very well keep pace with a jeep.

One of the officers looked at Sergeant Zeigler. "Grab a dozen men and accompany us."

The noncom nodded and swiftly selected the 12, and they all promptly climbed into a convoy truck that was parked under the spreading limbs of a huge oak.

"Where the hell is the driver?" the officer demanded.

Yama saw his chance and automatically took it, creeping through the brush to the base of the tree. A peek around the trunk confirmed no one had noticed. Slinging the Wilkinson over his left shoulder, he leaped into the air and caught hold of a low, stout limb. In a twinkling he was in the tree, his body flush with the bole. Climbing even higher proved easy, and soon he was level with the top of the convoy truck.

"Where the hell is the driver?" the officer repeated testily.

Risking another peek, Yama saw no one gazing in his general direction. The row of trucks effectively screened the oak from most of the Technics. He slid around the trunk and perched on the thickest of the limbs extending out over the vehicle. Well aware a misstep would plummet him to the hard ground 24 feet below, he extended his arms for balance, and went along the limb until he stood a foot above the canvas canopy stretched over the bed.

"Here I am, sir," a man shouted off to the left.

Yama eased down, grabbed the limb, wrapped his legs

around it, and inched lower until he hung upside down with his back almost touching the canvas.

"About damn time, Private," the officer barked. "Get in that cab and follow us."

"Yes, sir."

Yama tensed, heard a door open and slam shut. The engine coughed and roared to life and the manual transmission ground into first gear. Not yet, he told himself.

Like a rumbling prehistoric mammoth rousing itself from slumber, the huge truck began to go forward.

At that instant, when Yama hoped the soldiers in the bed would be gazing out the back at the comrades they were leaving or simply conversing or doing *anything* but looking overhead, he sank onto the canvas and lay perfectly still. The bed vibrated as the driver shifted again and the canvas swayed slightly. Could they see the outline of his body from below? Yama wondered. If so, a short burst from a Dakon and he could forget about getting revenge for Alicia's death.

A jeep also pulled out, the higher whine of its engine in distinct contrast to the growling of the truck, and took the lead.

Yama had to guess the sequence of events. The truck suddenly braked, and then the jeep was driving past them, heading in the opposite direction. It must have made a U-turn, he deduced, and received confirmation the next second when the troop transport did the same thing. Which made sense. The parked vehicles had been facing due west, and the city was due east.

His body bounced slightly whenever the truck hit a rut or a pothole, and there were quite a few of those. He twisted his head and saw the sun hovering at the rim of the horizon. It wouldn't set for another half-hour to 45 minutes, depriving him of the darkness that would greatly facilitate his task. Where was an eclipse when a person needed one?

The ride took less than two minutes, and only because the vehicles traveled at the sedate speed of 25 or 30, perhaps to convserve fuel.

Yama stared eastward and saw the 15-foot-high mesh fench stretching north and south for as far as the eye could see. Four strands of razor-sharp barbed wire capped the barrier. When they were closer, and before the angle prevented him from seeing the fence at all, he distinguished the peculiar metal globes imbedded in the mesh at ten-yard intervals, and remembered Blade telling him those globes were precision voltage regulators used to control the one million volts of electricity pulsing through the fence. If a person were to merely tap his finger on the fine metal strands, he would be fried to a charred crisp in seconds.

The head Warrior had told Yama about another barrior just inside the fence. A green belt 250 yards wide contained lush grass and beautiful flowers, deceptively concealing the thousands of sensitive mines buried inches under the surface.

Those Technics never missed a trick.

Both vehicles drew closer to the gate, and Yama suddenly discovered a flaw in his improvised strategy. Blade had informed him there was a guard tower inside the fence on the left side of the road, but his friend had said nothing about the tower being 30 feet in height. Any of the four guards typically manning the tower would readily spot him. He frowned, studying the large, clear plastic windows rimming the top. Only one trooper was visible, working at computer terminal. If the man didn't look up, Yama would be all right.

The truck slowed, evidently following the example of the jeep.

"Open the gate!" the officer yelled.

Yama heard voices, and then the truck lurched to a complete stop.

"Is that you, Major Crompton?" someone asked.

"Of course it's me, Kurt, you idiot. Now open the damn gate."

"Yes, sir."

Hinges squeaked as the order was obeyed.

"We're in a hurry so we'll dispense with procedure," Major Crompton declared.

Yama had his eyes glued to the tower. The soldier at the terminal was engrossed in his work. Good. Then he heard the gate guard speak again and his pulses quickened.

"Sorry, sir, but you know the rules. We have to check every vehicle that enters from top to bottom."

CHAPTER
SEVEN

"It would have been nice to sleep in a bed for a change," Hickok remarked. "The ground gets real old after a while."

Geronimo snorted and looked over his shoulder at the gunfighter. "You're becoming soft in your old age, Nathan."

"Who you callin' old, you mangy Injun," Hickok said. "I'm only thirty, the same as the Big Guy and you."

"True. But we look much younger, while your face bears a definite resemblance to a moldy prune."

"Have you ever tried to breathe with a gun barrel shoved up your nose?"

Still looking back, Geronimo had opened his mouth to offer a witty rejoinder when he inadvertently bumped into something as hard as iron, forcing him to halt. He faced forward.

Blade's gray eyes were narrowed in silent reproach and his brawny hands were on his hips. "Having fun?"

"What?" Geronimo blurted out.

"Are the two of you enjoying our little jaunt through the Outlands?" the giant said.

A sheepish grin curled Geronimo's mouth. "Am I to understand that you're ticked off at us again?"

"What do I have to be ticked off about?" Blade replied, and gestured at the forest bordering both sides of the narrow trail they were on. "Is it because you two morons insist on babbling like three-year-olds when we're out in the middle of nowhere and your voices could draw wild animals or mutations like manure draws flies?"

"Your comparison leaves a little to be desired," Geronimo protested.

"Yeah," Hickok said. "Our voices don't draw flies."

"Will you shut up while we're behind?" Geronimo asked.

Frowning, Blade wheeled and resumed their trek. "I can't recall exactly when, but the two of you definitely lost it a while back. I think it was after our trip to Houston."

"Lost what, pard?"

"Your sense of discipline. Belive it or not, at one time both of you were regarded as superbly disciplined Warriors."

"We still are," the gunfighter declared.

"Only in your dreams. Oh, sure, in a pinch you perform exceptionally well, and there's no denying you're two of the best Warriors in the Family, but you just don't know when to clam up. And frankly, your nonstop chatter can get on a person's nerves."

"We don't go overboard and you know it," Geronimo said. "Why don't you admit the real reason you're so uptight."

"Which is?"

"Yama."

Blade stared at the ground, his wide shoulders slumping.

In his heart he knew his friend had hit the proverbial nail on the head. Yama's unauthorized desertion of duty had caused Blade many a sleepless night, had troubled him to the very depths of his soul. Initially he kept asking the same question over and over again: "How could you?"

In the 106-year history of the Warrior class, there had been few who'd betrayed their trust in any respect. Hickok's own AWOL incident had been different, not as severe, because the gunfighter had gone to save a reckless youth from certain death and had left a note explaining his departure and promising to return. Everyone had known Hickok would leave, even the Elders who had cautioned him to remain at the Home. Everyone knew there was no stopping the gunman once he made up his mind about something.

Yama, however, had not bothered to leave a letter of explanation. He'd not told a living soul that he intended to depart. He'd simply failed to show up for guard duty when the Warrior Triad to which he belonged was scheduled for a shift.

The moment Blade had been informed of Yama's absence, he'd known where the errant Warrior had gone. Technic City. He'd chided himself for not seeing it coming, for not taking Yama aside and discussing the torment that had been eating at the man's insides ever since Alicia Farrow's death.

Maybe I'm partly to blame, Blade reflected. As head Warrior it was his job to monitor the others, to be there when they needed him. The organizational structure of the Warrior class had been designed with simplicity in mind, allowing for an efficient chain of command and the ready detection of personal problems, so he couldn't fault the system. The eighteen preeminent fighters were divided into six equal Triads; it couldn't be any simpler. And although he didn't work with other Triads on a daily basis except in a crisis, they attended briefings every morning when he was at the Home, and they frequently trained together under his supervision. He should have been sensitive to Yama's turmoil and been there when the man needed him the most.

The way Blade saw it, he'd failed. In a way he was as much at fault for the stain on the Warrior's record as Yama. Any honored position of leadership entailed certain obligations to those being led. A helping hand at a critical time was just one of them. He clenched his fists in annoyance at himself, and felt relieved when the gunfighter made a comment that curtailed his reverie.

"It'll be dark soon, pard. How long before we make camp for the night?"

"Soft, soft, soft," Geronimo muttered.

Blade gazed at the trail ahead. It stretched far into the distance on a southeasterly bearing. "As soon as we find a suitable spot," he answered.

"Which one of us bags supper?" Hickok asked.

"I believe it's your turn," Blade noted.

"And try to do better than a few measly chipmunks this time," Geronimo stated.

"I've never blown away sweet little chipmunks," Hickok declared indignantly.

"Oh. That's right. They were squirrels."

For 20 more minutes they pressed onward, until the trail unexpectedly bisected a narrow paved road running from east to west. Dotted with potholes and lined with countless cracks, buckled in sections here and there, the road was typical of those found in the Outlands.

"We'll camp here," Blade announced.

Geronimo regarded the site critically. "Wouldn't we be safer at a secluded spot in the forest?"

"We should be all right if we keep a big fire going," Blade responded, and nodded at the sun dipping below the horizon. "Besides, we don't have much time before dark. We'll just have to make do."

"I'll get the wood," Geronimo volunteered. He moved into the trees, picking up suitable fallen branches.

"And I'll go fetch us some grub," Hickok said, walking northward.

Blade watched them for a moment, then scoured the road in both directions. Nothing else moved. A stand of saplings to the left appealed to him; the trees would provide shelter from the winds that frequently arose at night, and give them a ready place to take cover should it become necessary. He walked over to the stand to set to work collecting leaves and twigs for use as kindling.

Geronimo returned bearing a load of limbs that he deposited with a loud crash. He went to go seek more, then paused. "There's some kind of building off to the southwest."

Looking around, Blade spied the vague outline of a two-story structure well back in the trees several hundred yards away. He wanted to kick himself for not spotting it first, and attributed his lack of alertness to his preoccupation with Yama.

"Want me to go see if it's occupied?" Geronimo volunteered.

"We'll check it out after Hickok gets back."

They attended to setting up their camp. In short order Blade had a crackling fire going and he and Geronimo squatted on their haunches next to it. The dancing flames pushed back the gathering twilight and produced shadows that writhed all about them.

Looking into the woods, Geronimo frowned and asked, "What do you think is keeping that dummy? He doesn't usually take this long."

"I don't know," Blade answered thoughtfully. "There hasn't even been a shot yet."

The leaden minutes dragged past.

"Maybe I should go hunt for him," Geronimo proposed.

"Worried?"

"About Hickok?" Geronimo rejoined, and snorted. "Don't make me laugh. I'm just hungry. Aren't you?"

Grinning, Blade stood and unslung the Commando. "Let's go find him together."

Into the gloomy forest they went, treading softly, and traveled on a northerly heading for a quarter of a mile. The woods had become eerily quiet; not so much as a bird chirped or an insect buzzed.

"I don't like this," Geronimo whispered, his FNC leveled.

"Me neither," Blade confessed, and cupped a hand to his mouth to shout as loud as he could. "Hickok! Where are you?"

Only the whispering breeze responded.

"Maybe the yo-yo got lost," Geronimo said, and bent his head back to yell, "Hickok! Fire a shot if you hear us!"

No retort followed the request.

"We'll go a little farther," Blade proposed. He led the way, weaving among a sea of tree trunks and thickets, and eventually came to the base of a knoll. From the top they would have an unobstructed view of the surrounding countryside, and with that in mind he ascended until he stood in a circular clearing at the very crest.

The sun had sunk from sight long ago. A full moon hung perched in the east and stars dotted the heavens. Their campfire was a small beacon in the night, steadily dwindling as the flames consumed the fuel.

"Hickok!" Blade bellowed several times without receiving a reply.

"Just between you and me, I'm getting worried,"

Geronimo said. "He's got rocks for brains, but even *he* wouldn't pull a stunt like this deliberately."

Blade was inclined to agree. "Use your revolver and fire three shots into the ground."

Nodding, Geronimo drew the Arminius, pointed the barrel straight down, and thumbed the hammer three times. The booming discharge seemed to echo out across the interminable forest.

Only silence ensued.

"We should separate," Geronimo recommended. "We can cover more territory that way."

"No," Blade said. "We stay together. If something—or someone—did get him, we could be next."

"But he might be wounded, unable to call out."

"No," Blade stressed, scanning the woods hopefully.

Geronimo's anger surfaced in his words. "I never thought I'd live to see the day that *you* would desert another Warrior."

"You're overreacting. I'd never desert a Warrior and you know it. But we can't go rushing off recklessly. Remember the rules we were taught," Blade said, and quoted the Elder responsible for most of the training novice Warriors received. "In combat or any potentially life-threatening crisis, the person who loses his head is himself lost. It's difficult to do, but when danger arises a Warrior must keep a cool head, must let calculated logic dictate his or her actions and not raw emotions."

"I remember the teachings vividly," Geronimo stated. "And the Elder mentioned there are exceptions to the rule."

"Sure," Blade agreed. "When you're in a fight for your life against hopeless numbers, then going berserk might be your only option. Or when a loved one is in danger, quite often emotion wins out over the mind. But neither of those instances qualify here."

Geronimo frowned. "I can't believe we're discussing elementary martial philosophy when our best friend might be lying at death's door."

"Don't you think I want to find him?" Blade snapped. "But what good would it do us to wander around in the dark for hours on end? We'd never find his tracks now. Our best bet is to wait until morning and and set out at first light."

"Logic tells me you're right," Geronimo conceded. "But my heart wants me to run through the woods screaming his name until I drop."

Blade started down the knoll. "If it's any consolation, I want to do the same thing."

"Mind if I try one more time?"

"No," Blade said, pausing. "Be my guest."

The one time turned out to be a dozen as Geronimo rotated in different directions and shouted the gunman's name over and over.

A mocking silence engulfed them.

"Let's go," Blade urged.

They were subdued on the return trip. Neither spoke until there were only a hundred yards to be covered and they could see the fire, which had not quite gone out.

"Maybe I was wrong. Maybe this *is* Nathan's idea of a practical joke," Geronimo suggested. "Maybe he's waiting for us now, laughing himself silly."

"If he is he'll be laughing out of a mouth that doesn't have any teeth," Blade pledged, partly in jest. He stared at the flames, hoping against hope Geronimo was right, but knowing in his soul that wasn't the case.

Something suddenly ran in front of the fire from right to left, gone almost as quickly as it appeared.

"Hold it," Blade cautioned, crouching and training the Commando on their camp.

"What is it?" Geronimo whispered, imitating the giant's actions.

"We've got company."

Again the flickering flames were momentarily obscured by something dashing past the fire.

"I saw it," Geronimo declared.

"Stay frosty," Blade said, breaking into a run, swerving from side to side to minimize the target he presented in case the visitors were human and possessed guns. He realized he wasn't swerving wide enough, though, seconds later when he heard a distinctive swishing noise and a long, thin shaft lanced out of the night into his right shoulder.

CHAPTER
EIGHT

Yama placed his right hand on the Smith and Wesson and steeled himself for the inevitable. If the guard climbed up to survey the canvas top, he'd have to fight his way in.

The voice of Major Crompton cracked like a whip. "We're in a hurry. This man is to be taken directly to the Central Core for a meeting with the Minister. If you want to go by the book and delay us, then go right ahead."

"The Minister?" the guard repeated in abject awe. "I didn't know."

There was a shuffling sound.

"I don't see anything underneath the truck," the guard declared, "and there's no way an animal or mutant could climb on top. So go ahead. We'll skip the thorough search this time around."

"Wise decision," the major said.

Relaxing, Yama listened to the jeep pull forward, and then the convoy truck did likewise. Several of the men in the bed were laughing. He slowly rolled onto his stomach and inched to the edge. Phase Two had been successful! Now came Phase Three.

On both sides of the truck was the deceptively serene green belt. Flowers were in full bloom and the grass a picture-perfect carpet of lush green.

Flowers in January? Yama was puzzled until he recalled Atmospheric Control Stations maintained mild climatic conditions in Technic City 12 months of the year.

The green belt soon gave way to a residential sector. Unlike traditional homes that were made of brick or wood, these in Technic City were composed of a unique synthetic substance. Marked by a wide diversity of bright colors and shapes, they were each one story high. Even the windows were tinted in different shades. Small lawns at the front and back of each house were meticulously maintained.

Yama saw only a few residents outside and wondered where the rest were.

The truck passed a checkpoint consisting of four soldiers and kept going. After a mile of practically deserted homes, an intersection appeared manned by more guards. Beyond them was a scene out of a madman's nightmare.

In three directions the roads were crammed with vehicles, primarily thousands upon thousands of three-wheeled motorcyles, trikes painted every color in the rainbow: red, yellow, purple, blue, brown, and more. There were also some four-wheelers, jeeps, trucks, and even a sprinkling of large sedans. They formed a raucous, flowing river of mechanized motion.

Yama marveled at the sight. The description he had heard didn't begin to do the bedlam justice. The sight jarred his memory, and he remembered Blade informing him that the Technics relied so extensively on trikes because their access to natural resources was limited and they couldn't afford to mass-produce full-sized or even compact cars.

The jeep and the truck went straight, making for the heart of the city.

That was when Yama spied it, far in the distance, gleaming in the golden glow from the setting sun.

Where once had been Logan Square, there now reared the headquarters of the autocratic elitists who were bound and determined to spread their tyrannical influence over the rest of the U.S. Appropriately named the Central Core, the governmental center was an architectural wonder. Ten stories high, it resembled an ancient Egyptian pyramid. It was two acres wide at the base and rising to a tapered point, and its sides consisted of scintillating crystal that sparkled as brightly as its gold-trimmed doors and windows. The whole effect dazzled the senses.

Yama's attention was diverted as the troop transport passed through the industrial and manufacturing sector. Also constructed from the special synethetic, the factories were all four stories high and either white, gray, or black. In contrast to prewar industries, these were sparkling clean, quiet, and environmentally safe.

A new danger presented itself. Yama realized that anyone standing at an upper-floor window would easily spot him and probably notify the authorities. His position was no longer tenable. But what could he do until the truck stopped? If he leaped down now he'd land in the midst of the bustling trikes.

He resigned himself to staying where he was and hoped luck would be on his side. On top of one of the buildings on his right appeared a billboard, and he read the advertisement displayed with interest.

"WINDY'S. TEN LOCATIONS TO BETTER SERVE YOU. ENJOY A SMILE MEAL FOR ONLY $14.95. A SIDE OF FRIED WORMS IS ONLY $1.75.

WINDY'S, WHERE YOUR STOMACH IS OUR BUSINESS.''

Yama had eaten worms once on a survival test. Every Warrior who wanted to graduate from the training program and advance to the status of active duty had to first pass the endurance trial. Escorted miles from the Home by an Elder, they were left with just their weapons and given a limited amount of time to safely reach the compound. The survival tests were invariably conducted in the hottest summer months, adding to the difficulty. On his, which he had completed in near-record time, he'd subsisted on grubs and worms for snacks. He could have easily slain a deer or other animal, but the delay would have cost him an hour or more each time he ate and he'd wanted to surpass the man who held the record: Blade.

The thought made him frown. His fellow Warriors were bound to be extremely upset over his departure, none more so than his good friend. The Elders must have been appalled at the news. If he returned, he undoubtedly faced the prospect of being stripped of his rank and possibly exiled from the Family. What a high price to pay for revenge!

Yama shook his head, dispelling the morbid introspection. He glanced at the billboard again, recalling the intelligence previously uncovered concerning the Technics' bizarre taste in food. With millions of people cramming the metropolis, the early leaders of Technic City had been hard pressed to keep everyone fed, until one of the top administrators hit on the original idea of using a plentiful food source that existed right under their noses, so to speak. Perhaps, Yama reflected, he'd try some if he had the opportunity.

Another billboard emphasized the cultural acceptance of the unusual dish: ''LARSON'S WORM FARM IN

MORTON GROVE. FIVE ACRES OF SCIENTIFI-
CALLY CULTIVATED SPECIMENS. PLUMP.
JUICY. NINE INCHES AVERAGE. GOVERNMENT
INSPECTED. RETAIL OR WHOLESALE. CALL
800-W-O-R-M FOR DETAILS.''

The Warrior twisted his head, listening to the strident
din of the congested traffic. Both the jeep and the truck
were creeping along at little better than 20 miles an hour.
He poked his head out and saw trikes and four-wheelers
packed close together.

One of the four-wheelers was riding abreast of the
truck's rear wheel. The driver, a hefty man in his early
twenties dressed in a brown uniform, yawned and
consulted a watch on his left wrist.

Inspiration struck, and Yama made sure the Wilkinson
hung snugly over his shoulder before he clutched the rim
of the canvas and braced himself. Other drivers were
bound to see his next maneuver, but it couldn't be helped.
If all went well, he'd be down a side street and lost in
the maze of buildings before the police arrived to check.

The four-wheeler slowly pulled forward, the driver
engrossed in maintaining a straight course and never once
looking up.

Yama gazed ahead. A block away was an intersection
dominated by a traffic light suspended over the center of
the junction. He'd seen such devices in the Civilized Zone
and knew they regulated the traffic flow. Currently the
light shone green. He watched it intently, hoping for a
change.

When the truck still had half the block to go, the traffic
light blinked to yellow, then red, and all the vehicles
crawled to a stop.

Yawning again, the driver of the four-wheeler braked
his machine a few feet from the center of the bed.

Thank you, Yama thought, and crawled a foot to the

left, bringing himself directly over his target. There was no time to lose; the light would change at any second. He slid outward, using his wrists to propel his body over the edge, and dropped down with his legs spread wide to land on the cushioned seat behind the driver.

The man involuntarily jumped when his vehicle bounced and glanced over his right shoulder. He had black hair and brown eyes that widened in amazement. "What the hell! Where did you come from?"

"Never mind," Yama said. He became aware of other drivers gaping at him.

"Never mind?" the driver repeated. "Mister, I don't know who you are, but you'd better get off my vehicle this instant."

"Unfortunately, I can't comply," Yama informed him, and surreptitiously drew his survival knife. He pressed the point into the guy's shirt and lowered his voice. "Do you want to die?"

Blinking, the man looked down and gulped. "No. Of course not," he answered weakly.

"Whether you live or not depends on how well you cooperate."

"What is it you want?"

"At the intersection take a right."

"No problem. Just don't kill me. Please."

Yama saw the light go green and he nodded. "Pull out and pay close attention to your driving. I don't want to attract the interest of the authorities."

The driver ran his eyes over the Warrior's outfit, then faced front and accelerated as the traffic flow resumed. He darted into the far right lane and hung a right at the junction.

Looking back, Yama saw no sign of pursuit. The jeep and troop transport were proceeding toward the Central Core.

"Who are you?" the driver asked over his shoulder.

"My name is unimportant."

"Where are you from?"

"You ask too many questions."

"Sorry."

They cruised into a business district. A variety of shops and large stores lined both sides of the street and there were more pedestrians than anywhere else. The traffic was thick and noisy.

"Are you in the military?" Yama inquired in the man's left ear.

"No," the driver replied. "Why would you think that?"

"Your uniform."

The man chuckled. "I work for S.P.D."

"Which is?"

"Speedy Parcel Delivery."

"You deliver packages?"

"Packages, mail, postcards, everything. S.P.D. is the biggest parcel delivery service in the city. You've probably seen our pink trucks driving all over the place."

"No," Yama said. He spied an alley not far off.

The driver fidgeted. "You don't know about S.P.D.? Then you must not be from Technic City."

"I'm not." Yama tapped the man on the shoulder and pointed at the alley. "Drive in there."

"I can't. My permit doesn't include alley privileges."

Yama dug the knife in a shade deeper. "It does now. When I give you an order, follow it."

"Yes, sir," the Technic responded. He slowed, used his turn signal, and when several pedestrians paused to grant him access, complied with the big man's request.

The alley connected one block with another. Halfway down it, on the right-hand side, were two huge trash bins spaced ten feet apart.

"Pull in between those," Yama directed.

Deftly manipulating the handlebars and shifting down, the driver brought the four-wheeler to an abrupt stop, nearly crashing into the wall in his nervousness.

"Turn off your machine."

The man promptly obeyed.

Yama slid off the seat and checked the alley to see if anyone had trailed them. Satisfied he had temporarily eluded detection, he sheathed the knife and motioned for the Technic to stand.

"What are you planning to do with me?" the man asked, and elevated his arms without being told.

The Warrior studied his prisoner's delivery uniform intently. It appeared to be several sizes too short for his frame but would serve to conceal him in a crowd. "Are you wearing underwear?"

Gasping, the Technic placed a hand to his throat. "I knew it! You're a pervert!"

"What?"

"I know all about your kind. There have been five or six reports on the news in the past year alone about the sick atrocities people like you commit."

"You're an idiot. Take off your uniform."

"Do what?"

Yama drew the Smith and Wesson. "I won't repeat myself again. Take off your uniform and be quick about it."

His hands shaking, the Technic removed his shirt, then his shoes and pants, exposing a white T-shirt and underwear. He crossed his hands over his crotch and turned sideways. "Now what?"

"Close your eyes."

"Oh, no," the man whimpered. He did as requested, his entire body trembling. "Please don't kill me. Please. Please. Please."

Yama stepped in front of him. "When you revive, you might benefit from looking up the word 'courage' in a dictionary."

"Huh?"

The Warrior planted his left fist on the tip of the guy's chin, not even bothering to use all of his prodigious might.

The tap sent the Technic stumbling back into the wall, his arms sagging at his sides. He sank to the ground, a ludicrous grin creasing his face, blood trickling from his lower lip.

Sighing, Yama began to pick up the man's shirt when the loud rumbling of a large engine alerted him to the fact a vehicle had just entered the alley.

CHAPTER
NINE

The force of the shaft slamming into him caused Blade to jerk to the right and nearly fall. He grunted, gritted his teeth, and crouched, staring at his shoulder to find an arrow protruding from his leather vest.

Geronimo also halted. He squeezed off a short burst, the FNC shattering the stillness, the barrel pointing to the southeast.

Pain engulfing his shoulder, Blade gripped the Commando in his left hand and tried to spot their attackers. He glimpsed an indistinct figure dashing off through the trees dozens of yards off. "Take cover," he stated, and moved toward a pine tree on his right.

Backpedaling, Geronimo swept the FNC from side to side, ready to cut loose at the first hint of hostility. No more arrows were fired. He stayed close to the giant until they were screened by the pines, then squatted and slid around to inspect his friend's wound. "The tip is sticking out about two inches."

"I know," Blade said, doubling over. He could feel

blood dampening his skin all the way down to his belt.

"Do you want to take it out now or wait?"

"Hold the tip steady," Blade responded, placing the Commando on the ground. He gripped the thin wooden shaft with his left hand.

"Are you sure you don't want to wait?" Geronimo cautioned. "The bleeding might get worse if you remove it."

"Can't be helped," Blade said, resisting waves of torment that washed over his mind. "We've got to go after them. They could know what happened to Nathan."

"You're the boss," Geronimo said, holding tight. "I'm ready when you are."

Licking his lips, Blade tensed his left arm, the huge muscles bulging, and abruptly bent his wrist, snapping the arrow in half. The movement aggravated the torment and he almost cried out. Inhaling, he said softly, "Your turn."

"Brace yourself," Geronimo advised, leaning the FNC against his leg. He wrapped both hands around the shaft as best he could, then heaved, extracting the arrow smoothly.

Nausea brought bitter bile to Blade's mouth, and he closed his eyes to ward off an assault of dizziness.

Dropping the blood-soaked shaft on the grass, Geronimo picked up the rifle and crouched. "Why don't you stay put and leave the chasing to me?"

"We stick together," Blade stressed, gingerly touching his shoulder, his fingertips becoming damp and sticky. He wiped them on his pants and retrieved the Commando.

"You're in no condition to be taking on anyone," Geronimo said. "And if you lose a lot of blood you'll be too weak to do either of us any good."

Blade stood with an effort, the veins on his neck

swelling. "Don't worry about me. Lead the way. I'll keep up."

"Sometimes you can be as hard-headed as Hickok," Geronimo muttered, rising and cradling the FNC. He warily surveyed the woods, then began moving toward their camp.

Keeping his right arm tucked against his abdomen, Blade stayed on his companion's heels. Both his front and back were sticky with blood. If the bleeding didn't cease soon he'd have to cauterize the entry and exit wounds.

Not a sound came from the surrounding vegetation. Their attackers apparently had fled when Geronimo cut loose.

Every few steps Blade's shoulder would experiencne an excrutiating spasm. He used the psychological training he'd received in preparation for becoming a Warrior to compartmentalize the pain, to suppress it by sheer force of will. To a degree the technique worked.

Most of the campfire had gone out. Those flames still reaching for the sky were only several inches high.

Geronimo reached it first and halted. "Look," he whispered, pointing at the ground.

Bending forward, Blade saw that many of the limbs used to make the fire had been pulled out and scattered about. Most bore red tips or tiny glowing embers. Had their attackers deliberately tried to extinguish the fire? It would have been smarter for whoever was responsible to leave everything as it was and set an ambush.

"Let's have a look at your shoulder," Geronimo proposed. He reached down and removed a short branch with flames rising from one end.

Reluctant to comply when there might be more bowmen lurking in the forest, Blade hesitated.

"Get on your knees," Geronimo said.

"What if we're jumped?"

"I doubt whether anyone is out there," Geronimo said, looking both ways along the road and then at the trees. "Even so, we both know what could happen to you if you don't let me examine the wound."

Clenching his fists against the pain, Blade did as the Blackfoot requested.

Geronimo scanned their vicinity once more, placed the FNC on the ground, then stepped up and gently lifted the right side of the giant's vest. He held the burning branch as near as he dared and frowned.

Tilting his chin, Blade saw the bad news for himself. A pencil-thin stream of crimson continued to seep from the entry hole.

"How do you want to do this?" Geronimo asked.

"We'll do it now before the fire goes out," Blade said, and began to remove his vest.

"The conditions aren't very sanitary. We don't even have any water."

"So we'll make do," Blade said, grimacing as he eased his left arm from the leather garment.

"Allow me," Geronimo offered. He slowly eased the vest off his friend's right shoulder, then set it aside. Moving behind the giant, he inspected the neat circle of pinkish flesh constituting the exit hole and announced, "You're bleeding here too."

"Then get it over with."

"Want to lie down?"

"No."

Geronimo leaned down, his eyes roving over the grass, and selected a piece of limb about six inches of length. "Here. Bite on this."

Nodding, Blade aligned the piece horizontally between his lips and clamped down hard, his teeth digging into the soft wood, which was still warm from the fire. The taste of charred bark filled his mouth.

"Are you ready?" Geronimo asked.

Blade nodded again.

Gripping the fireband firmly, Geronimo placed his left hand on Blade's shoulder to hold it steady, then began counting. "One. Two. Three." With a flick of his right wrist he speared the burning branch directly into the hole.

Unbelievable anguish racked Blade's shoulder and he involuntarily arched his spine and gasped. The pungent odor of burning flesh tingled his nostrils. He wanted to scream, but didn't, and thought he would bite clear through the wood.

After several seconds Geronimo yanked the branch away and smiled. "Looks good, if I do say so myself." He came around in front. "Let me heat this up and we'll have you cauterized in no time."

Blade wanted to tell him to hurry, that their attackers might return at any second, but he felt oddly sluggish, his arms dangling limply, the Commando lying at his side. He watched as the end of the branch was placed in the center of the fire and promptly burst into flames again.

Pivoting, Geronimo held the firebrand up. "It might be better if you closed your eyes."

Blade shook his head. He steeled himself, heard the three count, and looked at his shoulder just as the branch made contact. He saw the reddish-orange fiery fingers lick at his skin, heard the sizzling of his blood and flesh, and felt exquisite torment. Tendrils of smoke curled into the air. His teeth gnashed into the wood and he shuddered violently.

Geronimo grimly applied pressure for half a minute. Only when the skin around the hole had been burned black did he pull the branch away and examine his handiwork. "That should do it."

Swaying slightly, Blade opened his mouth wide and let

the charred limb fall out. He licked his dry lips and said, rather hoarsely, "Thank you."

"Any time. Just don't make it a habit of being shot with an arrow," Geronimo responded. He tossed the extinguished firebrand aside and reclaimed the FNC.

Weakness pervaded Blade's body and he struggled to regain his mental acuity. He tried to lift the Commando twice before he succeeded.

"You'd better rest a bit," Geronimo advised, his eyes alertly roaming in a circle, probing the sinister shadows. "I'll let you know if I see anything."

"Can't rest now," Blade mumbled. His brain sent the mental command to rise down his spine and along his nerves to his legs. Oddly, both limbs acted as if they were disembodied entities and didn't budge. Undaunted, and not a little furious at his body for its betrayal of his mind, he shifted the submachine gun to his right hand, put his left palm on the grass, and shoved to his feet, where he stood swaying, a mighty oak about to crash to the earth.

Geronimo took a tentative step, ready to grab the giant if necessary.

Blade languidly waved him off. He gripped the Commando in both hands and bent his neck to gaze at the awe-inspiring celestial display. Inhaling deeply, he felt renewed vigor slowly energize his body. Once the recovery process started, his strength returned swiftly. He donned the vest.

Far in the distance a wolf howled.

"Was that an omen?" Geronomi quipped.

Grinning, Blade looked at him and said, "Let's check out that house."

"Now?"

"Unless you have an urgent appointment."

Geronimo glanced at the giant's shoulder. "Why not give yourself more time?"

"Time is a luxury we can't afford. Whoever attacked us might have Hickok. Since that house is the only habitation we've seen for miles, logic dictates we check it out."

"Aye, Mr. Spock."

"Who?"

"Haven't you read those books in our library written by that Blish guy?"

Blade thought for a moment. The Family's Founder had constructed six enormous concrete bunkers at the Home, and in one of those Carpenter had collected hundreds of thousands of volumes of every conceivable subject. Aware that his followers and their descendants would require certain critical knowledge to survive in a world deranged by the ultimate insanity, Carpenter had devoted one of the largest sections in the Library to books dealing wth survival skills. Reference books on any and every subject had been amassed. Gardening books, hunting and fishing books, woodworking and weaving books were all included. There were volumes on natural medicine, on healing, on metal-smithing; on history, geography, and the sciences; and scores of books dealing with military tactics and strategies. To provide relaxation there were humorous books and novels by every fiction author who ever lived. Edgar Rice Burroughs was a perennial favorite, as was Roy Rockwood. The Warriors quite naturally showed a predilection for the many martial arts books and those related to various weapons. Blade had read all of the latter. Where fiction was concerned, he tended to restrict himself to a few favorites like Burroughs, Doyle, Fleming, and others. "I haven't read them," he confessed.

"They're in the science-fiction section."

"That explains it. I'm not much for farfetched fantasy," Blade said, and faced to the southwest. The inky forest effectively screened the house from his view.

"You should try them sometime," Geronimo suggested even as he constantly scoured the woods for danger. "There's this starship called the *Enterprise,* see, and a crew that's—"

"Geronimo."

"Yes?"

"Not *now.*"

"Oh. Sorry," Geronimo said, and sighed. "Boy, I wish Nathan was here."

"So do I," Blade stated, and started walking. With every stride he gained more confidence. Except for the agony in his shoulder, he felt fine.

The Warriors crossed the road and entered the woods beyond, moving quietly, fully professional now, staying side by side and dividing their line of vision, their combat-honed instincts primed. They covered two hundred yards without incident.

A twig snapped loudly to the west.

Both Warriors dropped into a crouch, their weapons swiveling, their ears straining.

A whisper of suggested movement came from the east.

Blade heard it and shifted, his back to Geronimo, his finger on the Commando's trigger. Was it coincidence? Or was someone trying to catch them in a pincer attack?

"I make out three on this side," Geronimo whispered.

A moment later Blade spied four figures darting from tree to tree 30 yards off, drawing the net tighter. "Four over here," he repeated.

"How did they know where we were?" Geronimo wondered.

"Doesn't matter," Blade said. "If they charge, waste them."

No sooner did the words clear his mouth than a series of bloodcurdling shrieks rent the night and the phantoms closed in.

CHAPTER
TEN

Yama's head streaked to the Browning and he stepped to the edge of the left-hand trash bin.

Driving slowly up the alley was a large white truck, a single occupant in the cab. Printed in block letters on the front of the huge, square hydraulic storage container was one word: SANITATION.

The Warrior pressed his back against the bin and calmly waited as the truck pulled in alongside the bins, the cab going ten feet past him, and braked. Evidently the driver had put the truck in park, because the door opened and slammed shut and the man started walking along the opposite side toward the rear.

Yama slid from concealment and cautiously moved in the same direction, listening to the driver happily whistle an airy tune. Pausing at the corner of the truck, he peered past it to see a well-built man over six feet in height who wore a white uniform.

The guy reached for a lever on the back of the truck.

In two quick paces Yama was next to him and jamming

the Browning into the man's ear. "Not a sound or you die."

To the sanitation worker's credit he didn't panic. His brown eyes widened and his mouth slackened, but he retained his composure and kept silent.

"Excellent," Yama said. "Come with me." He backed up, pulling the driver after him, until they stood between the trash bins.

The driver glanced down at the unconscious four-wheeler driver and the pile of clothes, and expelled a sharp breath.

"I won't harm you," Yama told him, taking a stride backwards in case the man decided to be a hero.

"What do you want?" the man asked.

"Is your truck a manual or an automatic?"

The significance of the query eluded the sanitation worker. His brow knit and he replied, "Manual, why?"

"No reason. Take off your clothes."

Defiance flared on the man's face for all of five seconds, until he stared long and hard at the unwavering barrel of the Browning. "Whatever you want, mister," he said reluctantly, and went about stripping off his uniform. Underneath he wore only orange underwear and purple socks.

Yama took a half-stride forward, his eyes on the white uniform, not giving the driver the slightest inkling of what was to come next. His left fist flashed straight out, his knuckles slamming against the driver's jaw and felling the man where he stood.

A hasty scan showed no one else in the alley, and Yama took but a minute to squeeze into the driver's white uniform, pulling it on over his own. He felt cramped and constricted with both uniforms on, with the sleeves on the sanitation outfit two inches too short and the hem of the pants two inches above his ankles, but resigned himself to wearing them. He wasn't about to remove the special garment constructed for him by the Family Weavers and run the risk of losing it.

Yama hurried around the front of the garbage truck and climbed into the cab, depositing the Wilkinson on the seat beside him. Some years ago he'd driven a jeep sporting a manual transmission, and he didn't think the truck would be much different. After studying the dials and knobs on the dashboard and the shifting diagram imprinted on the top of the gearshift, which had been left in neutral and not in park, he felt confident enough to get underway.

Tramping in the clutch, Yama worked the gearshift, hearing a loud grinding noise as he did. With minor difficulty he succeeded in getting into first, and he started down the alley.

A stream of humanity was crossing the sidewalk, barring the way to the street.

Yama pressed on the horn, producing a strident beep, and watched the pedestrians quickly get out of the way. The truck cleared the alley mouth and he took a right. According to the gas gauge he had three fourths of a tank, more than enough to meet his needs. He blended into the traffic flow, keeping in the far right lane in case he needed to make a rapid getaway.

He was glad the sanitation worker had shown up. The delivery driver's uniform would have been an even tighter fit, and he enjoyed greater anonymity in the truck than he would have on the four-wheeler.

But another problem presented itself.

The truck became hemmed in by scores of puttering trikes: front, back, and to the left. The drivers seemed heedless of their own safety and rode within inches of the truck's massive wheels, making the potential for an accident and subsequent chain-reaction smashups very high indeed.

Yama was hard pressed to keep from crushing another vehicle. His eyes were constantly in motion from side mirror to side mirror and out the windshield at the river of trikes and four-wheelers in front of him. Since a majority of the other riders had the disconcerting habit of braking at the last instant when a light changed to red, Yama was compelled to carefully monitor the taillights in front of him, his foot always poised to tramp on the brakes.

Three blocks were covered without mishap. Yama looked for a street running east and west, one that would take him in the general direction of the Central Core.

In the passing lane he saw a policeman on a trike.

Gluing his gaze to the side mirror, Yama watched the officer draw nearer to the truck cab. The policeman gave no indication of being in pursuit, and Yama maintained an appropriately blank expression, just like practically every driver he saw. To play it safe he dropped his right hand onto the Wilkinson.

Not even bothering to glance up, the officer cruised past the sanitation vehicle and continued on his merry way.

Yama let the cop get over a block ahead before he went about changing lanes, a hazardous procedure it its own right. Flipping on the turn signal, he had to wait for over a minute before the trikes behind him fell back sufficiently for him to change lanes. Once in the passing lane he accelerated to 30 miles an hour.

Up ahead appeared an intersection, the light green.

Again Yama employed the turn signal and slowed, preparing to swing to the east. Inexplicably, several trike and four-wheeler drivers commenced blaring their shrill horns. Mystified, Yama tried to figure out the reason but couldn't.

The opportunity to execute the turn came and Yama spun the steering wheel, swinging the gigantic vehicle to

the left, and not until the turn was completed and he saw
the wall of trikes before him did he realize his mistake.
He'd turned onto a one-way avenue *the wrong way*!
Automatically he slammed on the brakes and slewed the
truck to the left, trying to miss the startled riders who
leaned on their horns in frantic horror.

Yama missed the foremost row of trikes and brought
the truck to a lurching halt at the curb, his vehicle now
blocking the intersection. He went to throw the transmission into reverse, but a check of the mirror showed trikes
behind him.

More drivers applied their horns, creating a strident din.

Looking to his right, Yama spied the policeman coming
back. To the left was a military jeep bearing down on him.
Yama rolled down his window, letting them draw near,
planning to bluff his way out of the predicament. If he
made his move now, he might not live to reach the Central
Core, and reach it he must.

The officer got there first, halting near the truck's
passenger door and hurrying around the cab to demand,
"What the hell is going on?"

Smiling, Yama shrugged and put just the right amount
of irritation in his tone. "Beats me. One minute I was
driving along daydreaming about the meal I'm going to
eat at Windy's after I get off work, and the next thing
I know this heap of junk whips to the left all by itself.
I tried turning the wheel but there was nothing I could
do to stop it. Thank goodness I didn't run over someone."

"Sounds like your steering box went out on you," the
cop declared. "I'll call for a tow. In the meantime, try
to move it out of the intersection. Otherwise, you'll have
traffic blocked up for miles and I'll have to issue you a
ticket for obstructing a public artery."

"I'll try," Yama promised. "Can you clear those trikes
out from behind the truck?"

"Will do." About to hasten off, the patrolman paused when the jeep screeched to a stop and out jumped an army captain.

"What's going on?"

"I have everything under control," the policeman stated testily. "This guy's gear box is giving him problems."

"I'm Captain Herrick. We have an arms convoy coming along here in about five minutes and we can't afford any delays."

"Understood," the policeman said. He looked up at the Warrior. "Do as I told you," he ordered, and ran to the rear of the trash truck, where he began directing the traffic out of the junction.

Yama's curiosity was aroused. Both men envinced a slight nervousness at the prospect of the convey being stopped. Why? What difference could a few extra minutes make? He shifted into reverse, and when sufficient space presented itself he backed up and pointed the truck due south again.

The policeman ran over and called out, "How's it working now?"

"Seems to be okay," Yama responded.

"Good, but we can't take any chances," the cop stated, and looked to the north, as if seeking any sign of the convoy. "There's a parking lot fifty feet straight ahead. Nurse it there and a tow truck will arrive shortly."

"On my way," Yama promised, and pulled out slowly, watching in the side mirror as the efficient cop continued to direct the traffic. The military types waited on one side of the road, their impatience apparent.

Although tempted to keep on going and ditch the truck elsewhere, Yama drove to the almost vacant parking lot and pulled in. He leaned out the window and stared back at the junction. Almost immediately he spotted the convoy, consisting of six trucks, approaching at a brisk clip in the passing lane and using their horns to clear trikes and whatnot from their path.

The policeman had the intersection free of traffic, and all converging vehicles were stopped at the appropriate white lines to give the convoy unhindered passage.

Captain Herrick climbed in the jeep and it moved away from the curb to take the lead.

Still puzzled, Yama opened his door for a better view. From the west arose a distinct whomp! and a millisecond later the jeep exploded and was promptly engulfed in flames.

Spinning, the patrolman clawed for his service revolver, but a burst of automatic fire cut him in half.

The drivers of the convoy frantically braked, almost too near to the intersection to avoid it.

With the setting sun as their backdrop, three blue trikes roared down the sidewalk and closed on the first truck like wolves on a bear. Two men were astride each trike, all dressed in blue, and the back man on each carried a Dakon II. The gunners opened fire, pouring fragmentation rounds into the cab.

Yama saw the soldier driving the first truck dance and thrash about as the rounds perforated his body. Predictably, the truck slanted to the left, out of control, an enormous battering ram that plowed into the idling trikes and four-wheelers to the east and mowed them down in droves. The riders screamed as they were squashed and their vehicles reduced to so much scrap metal.

The men in blue swarmed around the second truck and repeated their maneuver. This time the truck lumbered to a halt in the middle of the intersection, the driver's bloody corpse leaning on the steering wheel.

Who were these guys? Yama wondered, and the obvious occurred to him. They must be with the Resistance Movement, and if so the implications were delightfully staggering. Because if the rebels in Technic City were this organized, this effective, then the Technics' days were numbered. He grabbed the Wilkinson and dropped to the asphalt.

Meanwhile the men in blue had taken out the third truck and were going after the fourth, which was in the act of grinding into reverse. The fifth and sixth convoy trucks were also doing clumsy U-turns, their ability to execute the about-face hindered by all the trikes around them and the confined roadway.

Yama ran toward the intersection. If he could link up with the Resistance Movement it would make his task a lot easier.

To the south arose the sound of engines whining at top speed.

Stopping, Yama whirled and spied four jeeps coming to the convoy's rescue, each conveying four soldiers armed with the inevitable Dakon. The jeeps were strung out in a line, using the shoulder of the highway, all the troopers intent on the conflict at the intersection.

The Warrior came to an instant decision. He ran to the road and started across, threading a path through the tightly spaced trikes, raising eyebrows and drawing shouts of alarm. But no one tried to stop him, and he burst into the clear when the foremost jeep was still 30 feet away.

One of the Technics saw him and pointed.

Dropping onto his right knee, Yama tucked the Wilkinson against his side and stroked the trigger, drilling the windshield with over a dozen holes and stitching the soldiers in the front seats with 9mm manglers.

Dead in the blink of an eye, the driver lost control and the jeep swerved into the vehicles on the highway, the collision loud enough to be heard for a mile.

One down, three to go. Yama rose and backpedaled as he fired at the second jeep, duplicating his success. This time the jeep went to the right, smashing into the side of a building.

Unfazed by the fate of their comrades, the remaining two jeeps never slowed.

Yama refused to give ground. He emptied the Wilkinson into the third jeep, which was 50 feet away and going at least 70 miles an hour, then drew the Browning and sighted on the driver. Before he could fire, however, one of the soldiers in the back straightened and hurled a spherical metallic object.

There could be no doubt as to what it was, and Yama spun and ran, taking several strides before he dove for the ground, knowing he was already too late a heartbeat prior to the near-deafening detonation. An invisible hand picked him up in midair and flipped him end over end with the force of a tornado. He tried to relax his body, to be ready to roll with the impact, but the next moment his head slammed into something as unyielding as steel and his consciousness fluttered into a void.

CHAPTER
ELEVEN

An arrow thudded into a tree trunk on Blade's right as he let the Commando rip and swung the barrel in an arc. He heard Geronimo's FNC chatter simultaneously.

Two of the charging figures were lifted from their feet and flung to the grass. The other two were unfazed, firing arrows as rapidly as they could notch the shafts to their bowstrings.

Blade heard an arrow buzz past his left ear and his lips compressed in anger. Not again, you sons of bitches! He tracked them with the barrel, and had the gratification of seeing both men go down, one convulsing and screaming.

The FNC ceased firing and Geronimo declared, "All down on this side."

Twisting, Blade probed the murky shadows for more bowmen. He distinguished the ominous black outline of the house approximately one hundred yards distant.

"Why were they using bows?" Geronimo whispered. "Anyone who wants a gun can usually find one in the Outlands if they're willing to pay the price."

"If more show up we'll ask them to use howitzers,"

Blade said sarcastically. He rose and cautiously advanced toward the last pair he'd downed.

Geronimo kept pace on the right. "Why are you in such a bad mood?"

"Oh, I don't know. Call me immature, but when someone shoots an arrow through me I tend to get a little ticked off."

They fell silent, and were soon standing over one of their dead foes.

"Ugly sucker," Geronimo commented.

Blade absently nodded.

The man was about six feet in height and quite lean and bony, his unkempt black hair down past his shoulders. A bushy beard rimmed his chin. He wore tattered jeans and crudely made sandals, nothing else. His skin was grimy, caked with dirt in spots; it appeared he hadn't taken a bath since birth. A deer-hide quiver hung on his back, and lying at his side was a stout longbow.

"All he needs is a loincloth and I'd take him for a caveman," Geronimo said.

They stepped to another body and found a man of similar height, weight, and general characteristics. Even the faces resembled one another.

Blade bent over for a closer inspection. There were enough similarities to lead him to suspect that the pair had been related, possibly even brothers.

"I hope Nathan didn't run into these guys," Geronimo said, scanning the forest.

"If he did, they might have taken him to the house," Blade said, and made toward it. In the back of his mind he doubted the gunfighter had been taken unawares by the bloodthirsty band. For one thing, Hickok's reflexes were the best of all the Warriors; at the slightest hint of a threat he could draw and fire faster than any human alive. For another, the gunfighter, like many of his combat-seasoned peers, had developed an uncanny sixth sense about dangerous situations. Catching him by surprise had rarely been done.

They crept to within 20 yards of the house without mishap. No more of the odoriferous bowmen appeared.

Blade halted in the shelter of a tree and studied the dwelling. There were no lights on within. The roof appeared to sag and the east wall slanted at an unnatural angle, suggesting structural damage brought on by a century of neglect and the ceaseless battering of the elements. A series of wooden steps led up to a narrow porch on which were a pair of rocking chairs. He glanced at Geronimo, who had crouched nearby, and motioned, starting forward with his Commando trained on the front door.

Not a sound came from the bowels of the once-stately residence. The wind rattled a few thin branches, the noise resembling the clattering of old, dry bones.

Pausing next to the bottom step, Blade listened while scrutinizing the blank, dark shapes of the windows. The glass pane in each had been broken out. He raised his foot to the third step, and frowned when the wood creaked loudly. In a rush he climbed to the porch and squatted.

Geronimo came up beside him.

Blade glided to the right of the door, and discovered it had long ago been torn from its hinges and now was lying on the floor just inside. He could barely make it out. The deepest cave in the depths of the earth would be hard pressed to match the near-total darkness inside. A faint, chill breeze seemed to be stirring the air, arising somewhere within.

After waiting a minute and not having anyone shoot at them or challenge them, Blade eased around the corner and placed his back against the wall.

Geronimo did the same, only he went to the left.

Now Blade had to wait longer, giving his eyes ample

time to adjust to the lack of light. When they had, all he could perceive were dim shadows. He speculated that it might be wiser to wait outdoors until daybreak and then go over every square inch of the house, but if Hickok had been captured, then every minute of delay was another nail in the gunfighter's coffin.

The room in which they found themselves contained intact furniture, which in itself was remarkably unusual. A sofa lined the far wall, and there were three chairs positioned randomly.

Blade stepped along the wall until he stood near a doorway. A hasty peek revealed additional furniture, a bed and a chair, their contours easily recognizable. He proceeded farther, and halted at the base of a flight of stairs.

Feet pattered on the floor above. Then all was quiet. Geronimo promptly joined his friend.

About to start upward, Blade glanced at the front doorway as a precaution, and was shocked to behold a thin form framed there, another of the bearded nocturnal prowlers armed with a bow.

The man was in the act of drawing the string.

Spinning, Blade punctured the bowman's chest with a short burst that smashed the guy onto the porch.

No sooner had the blasting of the Commando died away than the heavy pounding of feet heralded the advent of a newcomer on the scene, someone who raced downstairs heedless of the consequences.

Whirling around, Blade saw the person abruptly halt after rounding a bend in the stairs. He glimpsed swirling tresses and empty hands that were outflung in shock, and he barked a harsh, ''Freeze!''

Naturally, the woman turned and fled.

Blade took the lead and pounded in pursuit, taking four steps at a stride, his long legs lending him exceptional speed, and he was only a few feet behind her when she reached the next floor and tried to take a left. She slipped and fell to her knees, and he maximized her blunder by overtaking her and touching the barrel of the Commando to the back of her head. "I said freeze," he reiterated.

This time she obeyed, venting a terrified whine.

Looking up, Blade gazed along a narrow hallway. As near as he could tell it was empty.

Almost silently Geronimo stepped past the giant and the woman and covered the corridor.

"Who are you?" Blade demanded.

Another whine was the response.

"You must have a name," Blade snapped. "Tell me."

Haltingly, stuttering in fear, the woman answered, "Isabel."

"Isabel what?"

The woman had her head bowed and her long hair hid her face. She replied softly, her voice barely audible. "Isabel Kauler."

"Stand up," Blade directed, his ears tuned to detect any noises from below.

With as much enthusiasm as if she'd just been handed a death sentence, the woman stood, deliberately keeping her back to the giant and her head still bowed.

"Turn around."

As if she felt certain she was about to confront the worst ogre that ever existed, Isabel Kauler turned.

Blade inhaled and almost gagged. Like the strange bowmen, this woman evidently was ignorant of the fact that at one point along humankind's arduous evolutionary climb from the status of a lowly primate to a soul-endowed creation of a Supreme Spirit, a ritual known as the bath had been invented. "Where are the rest of your people?"

Isabel balked at answering.

"I'm in no mood to go easy on you," Blade warned.

"They fled," Isabel blurted out. "I'm the last one left."

"And you expect me to believe that?"

"It's the truth, mister. Honest. Cross my heart and hope to die."

"Why did you stay if all the rest ran away?"

"I wouldn't leave without my mate, Roth."

Geronimo cleared his throat. "This isn't exactly the best place in the world to interrogate her."

"I know," Blade said, acutely aware that they could well be trapped if the woman was lying and there were more bowmen outside. "You're coming with us," he declared, and seized her by the upper arm. Before she could react he headed down the stairs, and was extra vigilant as he neared the bottom. Thankfully the living room was empty, and he pulled her onto the porch.

The woman saw the corpse, and suddenly dug in her heels and tried to jerk free. "No!" she cried. "You've killed him! You've killed Roth!"

A twinge of guilt assailed Blade, a twinge he promptly dissolved by reminding himself it had been either Roth or one of the Warriors. He tightened his grip and kept going, hauling her after him.

Isabel tried to touch the body of her mate and stumbled, on the verge of falling, but the momentum of her captor swept her along, and she regained her balance in four or five ungainly strides.

Bringing up the rear, Geronimo constantly swiveled this way and that, knowing that slacking off for an instant might well result in making his lovely wife a widow.

Since employing stealth was impractical with the woman along, and since the bowmen had seemed to possess extra-ordinary night vision and would see them in any event, Blade took the direct route back to their camp. He counted on the presence of his captive to dissuade any of her fellows from attacking.

By the time they reached the fire the flames were nearly out.

"You can do the honors," Blade told Geronimo.

"Think it's safe?"

"I doubt they'll attack when we have one of their women," Blade noted, surveying the woods. "And besides, if Nathan *is* still out there, he'll need something to home in on."

Nodding, Geronimo knelt and swiftly rekindled the fire.

At the first bright flare of the hungry flames, Isabel Kauler recoiled and covered her eyes. She tried frantically to escape, twisting and tugging futilely, her strength compared to the giant's the same as that of a timid sparrow to a mighty eagle.

"What's wrong?" Blade asked her.

"The bright light hurts my eyes."

Perplexed and curious, Blade turned her away from the fire and stared at her face as she lowered her hands. He hadn't paid much attention to her eyes before; now he found they were pale, almost white in color, although her hair and eyebrows were a dark brown. Her filthy skin was exceptionally pale, as if she seldom if ever was abroad during the day. "Have you always been this sensitive to light?" he inquired.

Isabel nodded.

A disturbing insight prompted Blade to probe further. "And all of your people are the same way?"

"Yes."

"They only come out at night?"

"Yes."

"For how long has your clan be nocturnal?"

"Nok-what?"

"For how many years has your clan gone outside only after sunset?" Blade amplified his question.

"Since as far back as anyone knows."

Geronimo stood and glared at her. "What happened to our friend?"

"Who?" Isabel responded timidly.

"Hickok is his name. He wears buckskins and always packs a pair of Colts. Don't pretend you don't know who he is," Geronimo said.

"But I've never seen anyone like you describe."

"Bull, lady."

The venom in the Blackfoot's voice made Isabel take a step backwards. "Really. I don't know him."

"Maybe the men of your clan jumped him," Blade interjected. "They attacked us without provocation."

Isabel shook her head. "I'm sure they didn't."

"How can you be certain?" Blade asked doubtfully.

"Because they would have brought his body home for us to gut and hang from a tree."

The innocent simplicity with which she made the disclosure stunned Blade. He exchanged bewildered expressions with Geronimo, then inquired, "Why would you want to hang it from a tree?"

"How else can we drain the blood?" Isabel answered, her tone implying he must possess the intelligence of a rock.

Geronimo spoke, his voice gravelly. "Why would you want to drain the blood?"

"Blood can carry sickness. We're taught never to drink it or we might die. Then too, it's easier and a lot less messy to carve a body up after all the veins and such are dry."

Horrifying insight flooded through Blade. "Your clan eats other people?"

"Sure? Doesn't everybody?"

Before the Warrior could reply to her naive query, to the north arose the patter of someone running accompanied by the crackling of leaves underfoot, and Blade pivoted to see a figure charging directly toward them.

CHAPTER
TWELVE

Was he dead again?

He hoped so.

Yama seemed to be floating in a Stygian void. Total blackness engulfed him. He tried to blink to determine if his eyes were open or closed, but he couldn't feel his eyelids move. When he went to flex his arms and legs nothing happened. It was as if his consciousness, his very soul, no longer inhabited his organic body and now hung suspended at the core of an empty infinity.

It shouldn't be like this, he noted.

It hadn't been this way the last time.

The last time.

Vivid memories of Seattle washed over him with the force of a tidal wave. He recalled being shot with an arrow and taking shelter in an abandoned building. How bizarre it had been when he'd seemed to float out of himself and gazed down at his bloody form. Then there had been a flying sensation as he'd sailed through a long, dark tunnel into a realm of Utopian splendor. Some might have called it Heaven, others Paradise, still others Nirvana. To him it had been the sublime place where he'd encountered *her* again.

Lieuteant Alicia Farrow.

Once she had been a loyal Technic soldier sent to assist in destroying the Home and eliminating the Family. But then she'd committed the ultimate taboo and fallen in love with an outsider. With Yama.

He'd reciprocated, and savored every moment in her company. For the first time in his life he'd known genuine, profound happiness. The mere fact that a woman could love him, given his peculiar temperament, had astonished him. He'd felt their affection had been too good to be true; even so, he'd dared to envision a future with her constantly at his side.

Fate had decreed otherwise.

Alicia had died saving his life. Of all possible emotional burdens, the selfless, fatal sacrifice of a loved one had to be one of the hardest to bear. He'd rather have died than to have lost her.

But lost her he had.

Then came the trip to Seattle and the "Near-Death Experience," as one of the Elders later described it. His soul had joined her on whatever level of existence she now inhabited, and he'd enjoyed a fleeting taste of communion with her again. He would have stayed there forever, but such wasn't to be. A beautiful bright light had materialized to inform him it wasn't his time.

Of all the rotten luck.

So he'd reluctantly glided back through the tunnel and into his body, to awaken in a rejuvenated but melancholy frame of mind.

The baffling experience had changed him, transformed him somehow. Where before he'd done his utmost to avoid dying, and probably had secretly dreaded the event, he'd grown to expect death as merely the means of passing on from Earth to the next higher level. Death became a portal, a technique of translation from one plane to another. With the unshakable certainly that those who possessed but the faintest flicker of faith would survive came a newfound fearlessness, an almost fanatical belief in his own invincibility. He'd reasoned that even if his body was destroyed, he would survive.

For months he'd behaved as if no bullet could harm him, no knife end his life. He'd waded into the thick of battles without the slightest of qualms or cares. And always he'd emerged triumphant. His soul had pulsed with vibrant power.

Then he'd lost it.

Somewhere along the line he'd lost that special feeling. He couldn't quite pinpoint the exact moment, but by the time he took on the Technics again in Green Bay his regression had been obvious.

Why? Why? *Why?*

Did the aftermath of an NDE, that awareness of an inner glow and a sense of being endowed with surpreme wisdom, only persist for a limited time? Were the spiritually pure experiences of the soul somehow diluted by the body? He didn't know.

Oh, he'd resisted lapsing back into his old mind-set. He'd fought it, tried to artificially reproduce the feeling, to no avail. And when he finally admitted he'd lost the greatest treasure a person could own, an emptiness had pervaded his being. It was as if he'd been turned upside down and a crucial part of his personality had poured out, ever to be reclaimed again.

But he wanted to reclaim that feeling. He longed to know true inner joy again.

To compensate for the emptiness, he'd developed and nurtured a burning urge to repay the Technics for Alicia's death. Even though he'd met someone new, a lovely woman named Melissa who loved him as much as Alicia ever did, and even though a measure of happiness had returned to his life, he'd been unable to diminish his drive for vengeance.

By all rights he should have gone after the Technics when Alicia died instead of moping for months. He'd concocted 101 excuses to justify his failure: There were too many Technics; Technic City was too far; too much time had elapsed for the vengeance to have any meaning. They'd all been lame excuses.

Ultimately the strain had proven too much. He'd pondered the matter for weeks on end, and then simply left the Home and all those he cared for to satisfy his obsessive urge. He'd sacrificed his future as a Warrior to pay his debt to the past. He'd decided to topple the Technic government.

Perhaps he'd always known the task was impossible for a single man to achieve. Perhaps he'd eluded himself and carried through with the scheme because secretly he'd wanted to fail. How else could he rationalize the suicidal mission? One man against millions was laughable odds.

A new thought occurred to him, and he balked at acknowledging it: What if he'd hoped to die so he could rejoin Alicia? He had to admit the idea appealed to him.

Or did it go deeper than that?

Had a subtle death wish seized his soul because he yearned to journey to the next level again, because he had tasted Heaven and couldn't tolerate life on earth? The other side had been so peaceful, so indescribably wonderful, totally unlike the gritty reality of existence on planet Earth. Who wouldn't crave a steady diet of sterling perfection, sublime love, and exalted beauty after wallowing in the moral morass of mortal uncertainty?

Yama tried to turn his head but there was no head to

turn. *Where are you?* he tried to scream. Where is the tunnel and the light and Alicia?

I'm here.

Take me.

But he drifted along without a response. Where am I? he asked himself repeatedly. Is this another level? Is this the opposite of light and life?

Is this—Hell?

The idea jolted him. He'd never given much credence to the fire-and-brimstone sort of eternal damnation for wicked sinners, although the justice of the punishment merited his approval. Could this blank nothingness be Hell, or was there yet another level where raging cold flames tormented the souls of the degenerately evil? If so, where was he?

Wherever it was, once again the fact that a mortal's life didn't end at the grave was impressed upon him. The awareness invigorated him like a cold shower on the hottest of days, tingling his consciousness and renewing the long-lost feeling of cosmic awareness.

Once again he knew.

He knew!

With the knowing came a dizzying sensation as the black hole in which he floated abruptly collapsed upon itself and sucked him down with it.

First sense: hearing. There were muffled voices around him, men and women speaking in hushed tones as if they didn't want to wake him up. He catalogued their comments.

"Where can he be from?"

"I don't know, but he sure as hell isn't from Technic City."

"Why did he help us?"

"Who knows? I doubt we'll find out because the doctor doesn't think he'll live until morning."

Second sense: smelling. He registered the aroma of frying meat and boiling vegetables, spinach and corn.

Third sense: touch. He realized he was lying on his back on a hard surface, his arms at his sides. From the lack of weight in his holsters he deduced his weapons had been taken. Not nice.

"Here comes Falcone," said a man.

The soft tread of rubber soles announced the arrival of the newcomer and a deep voice asked, "Any sign of life yet?"

"No. The doc just checked him a few minutes ago. His heart is barely beating and his body temperature has dropped to critical levels. There's little hope."

"Damn. Too bad. He might have proven useful," Falcone said.

Yama heard the rustle of clothing and felt warm breath on his face. The one called Falcone must be examining him in the hope of detecting a spark of life. Why disappoint the man? He opened his eyes to find a rugged, dark-haired man intently regarding him, their noses almost touching. The man's blue eyes expanded in shock.

Someone gasped.

Time to rejoin the living, Yama reflected. His right hand swept up and clamped on Falcone's neck, and he surged into a sitting position. Under him was a metal table, and surrounding it were seven people wearing light blue uniforms, all armed. They were astounded by his revival and for five seconds no one moved except Falcone, who tried to wrench loose of Yama's grip but couldn't.

A blond guy drew a pistol and pointed it at the Warrior's head. "Let go of him!" he barked.

"Where are my weapons?" Yama inquired.

"Screw your weapons. Let go of Falcone," the guy repeated, and the others brought their own firearms to bear.

Yama started to slide from the table, still retaining his hold on the now furiously resisting Falcone. The man battered at Yama's arm, but the blows were barely felt.

"Don't move!" the blond guy cried. "We'll shoot."

"Be my guest," Yama said calmly, placing his feet on the tile floor. He straightened and squared his wide shoulders as more people in blue converged on him, forming a ring three or four deep. Beyond them spread a spacious chamber with lavender walls and a vaulted orange ceiling, comfortably furnished with four plush sofas and twice as many chairs.

"Let go of him!" a woman demanded.

"Where are my weapons?" Yama repeated, scanning their angry faces, noting an even mix of sexes and a range of ages from the late teens to the early sixties.

A white-haired man pushed through the ring, calling out, "Don't shoot. Don't anyone shoot." He halted in front of the Warrior and looked fearlessly up into the big man's eyes. "Please don't kill him."

"Where are my weapons?"

"We can't give them to you."

"You have no choice."

The man did a double take. "How do you propose to obtain them? You'll be dead before you take a step."

Yama let the corners of his mouth curl upwards and saw the chilling effect it had. "I can not die."

"What?" the white-haired man responded.

"You have until I count to ten to return my weapons. If you haven't done so, then the Resistance Movement will come to an abrupt, inglorious end."

"You know who we are?"

"One," Yama said.

"How do we know we can trust you?" the man asked.

"Two."

One of the men spoke up. "He's bluffing."

"Three."

"I don't think he is," someone else said.

"Four."

Falcone had both hands on the fingers squeezing his neck and was striving to pry them off. He sputtered, his knees sagging, and motioned wildly at the white-haired rebel.

"Five."

The blond guy took a step forward. "Let me blow this jerk away."

"Six."

"No!" the white-haired man declared.

"Seven."

Some of them tightened their grips on their weapons in expectation of firing.

"Eight," Yama said, holding Falcone upright with one arm and easing his grip just a bit so the man wouldn't die on him.

Nervously glancing from the Warrior to Falcone, the white-haired man gnawed on his lower lip.

"Nine."

"We'll do it!" the white-haired man exclaimed. "We'll give you your weapons."

Yama stopped counting and released Falcone. The rebel tottered, and would have fallen if others hadn't caught him. "I'm waiting."

"Get his weapons," the white-haired man directed.

"But Roy—" the blond guy began.

"Do it!" Roy snapped.

There was a commotion at the back of the band and two men came forward bearing the Warrior's personal arsenal, including all of his spare magazines, clips, and boxes of ammo, which they promptly deposited on the table.

Yama wasted no time in replacing the Browning, Magnum, scimitar, and survival knife in their respective holsters and sheaths. He picked up the Wilkinson, verified the magazine was still empty, and inserted a new one. The rest of the ammunition he crammed into his pockets. Then, nodding in satisfaction, he faced the rebels.

Falcone, supported by two men, rubbed his sore neck and rasped out, "Who *are* you?"

Smiling, Yama looked at him. "Think of me as the Angel of Death."

"Why are you here?"

"I'm going to help you topple the Technic government."

The blond guy snorted. "Oh? Just you and us, huh? And when are we supposed to accomplish this miracle?"

Yama glanced to the left at a window and noticed the stars in the sky. "At the first crack of dawn."

CHAPTER
THIRTEEN

The Minister stood in his office staring out one of the tinted glass windows at the myriad lights of the metropolis, his hands behind his back. A knock sounded and he called out, "Enter."

"It's me, sir," Ramis announced.

The Minister saw his subordinate's reddish reflection in the pane as Ramis walked up behind him. "What is the latest projection?"

"Major Langella says the gas-dispersal systems will be fully operational within three days," Ramis reported.

"I had hoped it would be sooner," the Minister remarked, pursing his lips.

"He told me they must triple-check the buildings for leaks. Should any of the gas escape and kill bystanders, someone might suspect the truth about the inoculation program. It would ruin the whole operation."

"I know," the Minister reluctantly agreed. "And considering the scope of the project, there's no room for mistakes. Tell the major to do his usual thorough job, but urge him to complete the installations within two days if at all possible.''

"Yes, sir," Ramis said, and turned to go.

"Oh. One more thing."

"Sir?"

"I wanted to compliment you on the excellent job you did with the Schonfeld tape. Not even an expert will be able to tell that those spools were doctored."

"Thank you, Excellency," Ramis said. "But if I may be so bold, I still believe you're taking a great risk if you formally accuse him of treason. He's one of the most patriotic officers in our military."

The Minister sighed. "I appreciate the risk, my friend, but this entire enterprise is fraught with risks. Selective genocide has seldom been attempted on such a massive scale. Exterminating a million and a half men between the ages of eighteen and thirty-five is any politician's worst nightmare. Simply working out the logistics has given me numerous headaches."

"Which reminds me, sir. All the press releases concerning the phony disease have been prepared for the media and are awaiting your approval."

"Good."

"We have a dozen physicians ready to authenticate the releases by calling a news conference and announcing the results of their so-called five-year study."

Turning, the Minister regarded his assistant intently. "I want your personal opinion, Ramis."

"Excellency?"

"Do you think it will work?"

"Of course, sir."

"Be specific."

Ramis pondered for a moment. "Very well. Since you've asked, I'll tell you that I firmly believe your devious scheme in brilliant. The problem confronting you was monumental, yet you selected an infallible way out. Sure, all the computer projections indicate there will be widespread revolt in Technic City in seventeen years, or possibly somewhat sooner. But you were astute enough to determine that the prediction only held true if the population growth continued at its present rate and there were no changes in our social order."

A wry smile creased the Minister's countenance. "You should be specific more often, my friend. Your insights are commendable."

"Will that be all?"

"Yes," the Minister said. Then he thought of one last item after all. "No. Not quite. What time is my appointment with the scientists from the Bioengineering Department?"

"Eight A.M. They were quite excited at the prospect of providing a personal demonstration."

"And they're actually bringing their Cy-Hounds here?"

"Yes, sir. I felt it more appropriate than for you to pay them a visit."

"I can always rely on you to have my best interests at heart," the Minister said. "Thank you, Ramis. This definitely will be all."

"As you wish, sir." Ramis gave a little bow and departed.

Grinning in amusement, the Minister waited until the door closed behind his faithful lackey, and then turned to the window. His grin transformed into a frown. If only he had Ramis's confidence in his own plan! But it *must* work. If it failed, the Technic elite would eventually be overthrown and Technic City would become the political equivalent of a cesspool: a democracy.

The idea had initially occurred to him shortly after the Warriors destroyed the Technic research facility at Green Bay. He'd optimistically counted on the fruits of that

research, which would have resulted in the capability of
literally controlling the minds of the populace, to prevent
the predicted revolution from ever materializing. With the
facility reduced to rubble, he'd been compelled to resort
to an alternate means.

Many sleepness nights had been spent in rejection of
one impractical idea after another before inspiration
struck. The computer had indicated that those most
susceptible to the false teachings of the Resistance
Movement were persons between the ages of 18 and 35,
and that it would be the males in that age range who would
be most likely to rise in violent revolution. Women would
play key roles naturally, but most of the actual fighting
would be done by the men.

But what if there were no men to take up arms?

That was the question he'd mentally posed, and the
answer had been a revelation. He'd realized he could
forestall the rebellion by eliminating those most likely to
rebel. Such a simple answer, and one that might have
eluded a lesser man of limited intellect.

Then came the nightmare. How to accomplish the deed
was the burning issue. He couldn't simply invite all able-
bodied males in the targeted age range to a mass
execution. More restless nights had been spent before he
devised a devious ploy.

The Minister chuckled as he contemplated the details
of his scheme.

First there would be an announcement that a strange
malady was striking the men of Technic City, a curious
disease that only afflicted those from their late teens to
their mid or late thirties. Much would be made of the
presumed selectivity of the virus.

The next step involved his panel of physicians and their
alleged research. They would speculate that the disease

was the work of a chemical warfare agent employed during World War Three. Perhaps the virus had been developed by the enemy in an effort to wipe out those men of prime combat-ready age in the former United States. Now, somehow, the virus had been introduced into Technic City.

There would be hysteria among the male population, no doubt. Calls would be made for massive government spending to find a cure. After a suitable interval of three or four weeks he would personally go on television and announce that a cure had been perfected, that it involved a simple inoculation, and that all those males in the high-risk group would receive cards in the mail advising them when to report for theirs.

Then huge warehouses would be converted into "health centers" where inoculations would supposedly be given. A fleet of trucks was being prepared to transport the incinerated remains out of the city. If all went well, the procedure would work just as smoothly as that employed by the Nazis when so many Jews were ushered into similar gas chambers and subsequently reduced to ashes.

In one day, from dawn until about midnight, a million and a half men would die. He'd wisely permit another 400,000 males of the same age group to live purely for future breeding purposes; killing all of them would present insurmountable difficulties later on. These men wouldn't recieve inoculation appointment cards for the fatal day.

At midnight the day of the extermination martial law would be declared. It would be claimed that the shots administered to the men were lethal. The Resistance Movement would receive the blame. Everyone would be told the rebels had managed to poison the serum supply.

The Minister laughed at the thought. What a terrific double stroke! He would reduce the numbers of those who

posed the greatest threat to a manageable level *and* brand
the Resistance Movement with the responsibility for the
atrocity.

Ramis had been correct.

He was brilliant.

Only one hitch yet remained. There were a few top-
ranking officers and politicians who might be inclined to
launch an investigation of their own into the affair, and
he intended to silence them before the project was even
launched. So far two prominent administrators and a
colonel had been indicted on trumped-up charges of con-
spiring with the rebels. Shortly he would go after bigger
game: General Julian Schonfeld, the man who posed the
greatest threat of all.

The Minister yawned and arched his spine. Soon he
must turn in. Only one last item remained to be considered: what was he to make of Corporal Lyle Carson's
assertion that a lone Warrior named Yama had launched
some kind of personal war against Technic City? And
what about the business of Lieutenant Alicia Farrow? How
the hell did she fit into the total picture?

He'd listened in barely disguised amazement to the
corporal's story. There had been no doubting it because
Carson had been under the complete influence of a potent
truth drug. Unfortunately, the new information raised
more questions than it answered.

Who was this Yama?

How could one man possibly hope to prevail over the
combined might of the Technics?

Were there other Warriors involved?

Was Yama's tale a fabrication to throw the Technics
off, and if so, off *what*?

The Minister turned and headed toward the door leading
to his opulent private quarters. Tomorrow he would

attempt to solve the riddle. At the moment he was too tired and needed sleep.

At least one aspect of the next day promised to be diverting. The demonstration of the Cy-Hounds should be of particular interest. He'd always been fascinated by biomechanical life forms.

An intriguing idea hit him.

If these Cy-Hounds were everything they were cracked up to be, he might keep a pair as pets. They'd be the ideal companions, less critical than a woman, more affectionate than Ramis, and able to rip the throat out of anyone who displeased him.

On second thought, perhaps he'd keep a half dozen.

CHAPTER
FOURTEEN

Blade swept the Commando up, his finger tightening on the trigger. At the last possible instant he realized the figure wore buckskins, and he tilted the Commando at the ground and declared angrily, "Hickok!"

Geronimo had the FNC to his shoulder. He lowered the weapon, beaming happily, and then quickly adopted a mean expression. "It *is* him. Darn. Here we thought we'd lucked out and some poor mutation was having a bad case of indigestion."

Almost out of breath, Hickok covered the final few yards and halted. He placed his hands on his thighs and bent over, inhaling deeply, his face flushed, staring at Isabel Kauler in surprise.

"Have you been out jogging?" Geronimo asked with a feigned air of utmost innocence. "It's about time you got a little exercise. You're getting a bit flabby around the middle."

"You wish," Hickok declared, reaching up to adjust the strap on his Marlin.

"Where have you been?" Blade inquired.

"Forget about me for a minute," Hickok said. "What was all that shootin' I heard? I thought you guys were in trouble, and I bet I ran five or ten miles gettin' here."

"More likely one or two," Geronimo said.

Blade nodded at the woman.. "We ran into a band of cannibals. She's one of them. Her name is Kauler, Isabel Kauler."

The gunfighter noticed the hole in the gaint's vest and the dried blood rimming it. "What the dickens happened to you?"

"I took an arrow," Blade explained. "But enough about us. Where in the world have you been?"

"After our supper."

"All this time?"

Hickok nodded and straightened, resting his palms on the butts of his Pythons. "Do you recollect all that ribbin' I was gettin' from Geronimo earlier about blowin' away chipmunks and squirrels?"

"Yeah. So?" Blade responded.

"So I decided I wasn't comin' back with anything less than a ten-point deer or an elk."

Geronimo snickered. "What did you do? Chase one to Canada?"

"Pretty near. I spied a small herd of elk and tried to sneak up on the critters, but they got my scent and lit out. Naturally I went after them. Before I knew it I came out of the forest onto the edge of a cliff, and down below in a small valley were the danged elk. Beats me how they get down there. I looked for a ravine or some other way to the bottom, but couldn't find any, so I climbed down."

"Let me guess," Geronimo interjected. "The elk picked up your scent again and took off."

"Yep. The blamed wind kept changin' direction on me each time I'd get almost close enough to use the Marlin,"

Hickok detailed. "Finally it got too dark for me to bother wastin' my time, and I figured I'd head on back. But going up that cliff without any light was next to impossible. Took me forever," Hickok related. "Then, when I finally did get back on top, I heard all this shootin' and came runnin' to help. End of story."

"Didn't you hear us calling you and firing shots before that?" Blade asked.

"Nope. I must have been down in the valley then."

Geronimo leaned toward Blade. "Tomorrow let me go after our supper. At least we'll have something to eat."

The gunfighter stared at the Indian for a second. Suddenly both of his hands became quicksilver, drawing and extending both Colts in Geronimo's general direction. Twin flashes flared from the barrels as twin blasts sounded simultaneously.

Blade pivoted, hearing the shriek of pain that greeted the shots, and spied two women armed with bows who had been creeping toward them. The pair had been crouched on the other side of the road, about to unload arrows. The gunfighter's shots had cored their brains and snapped them onto their backs.

No one spoke. The echoes of the gunfire died away. Isabel began crying softly.

"Friends of yours?" Hickok asked Geronimo, and twirled the revolvers into their holsters.

Blade took several strides and gazed at the bodies. Why had it been women this time? Were all the men dead? Next it might be kids. "We're getting out of here."

"Why, pard?" Hickok asked.

"Because I'm not keen on the idea of getting a shaft in the back in the middle of the night," Blade said. "We'll take the road east about a mile or so and camp there for the night."

The gunfighter shrugged. "If that's what you want. But

gettin' scratched by that arrow must have rattled your brain. Since when do Warriors run from scuzzy cannibals?''

"We're not running. We're engaging in a strategic withdrawal," Blade said.

"You mean there's a difference?"

The giant ignored the gunman and moved behind the woman. He gave her a nudge and said, "Start walking."

They headed out, Geronimo taking the point without having to be told and walking 15 feet ahead of his companions and their prisoner.

"Why the blazes are we bringin' her along?" Hickok inquired, his contempt barely concealed. "We should do the world a favor and put her out of her misery. No one will miss one lousy cannibal."

Blade glanced at him. "Sometimes you can be as hard as stone."

"Sometimes a Warrior has to *be* as hard as stone. Otherwise the cow chips will gain the upper hand."

"We're not executioners, Nathan. We're protectors of the Family and the Home. When we start setting ourselves up as the ultimate judges we've overstepped our bounds."

"If you ask me we're oversteppin' our bounds by lettin' a cannibal live. You know as well as I do that if she found one of the Family alone in the woods she'd likely knock them on the noggin and whip up a barbeque on the spot."

The truth of the gunfighter's assertion bothered Blade. "We'll decide what to do later," he proposed.

"Fine. But don't expect me to sleep anywhere near her. I don't intend to end my days as someone's late-night snack."

Blade fell silent, contemplating the dilemma. If he released her she'd undoubtedly go back to her revolting practice in no time. According to the Elders, many groups and individuals had reverted to cannibalism after the war.

The worst of it had occurred during the two decades immediately after Armageddon when the elevated radioactivity and the chemical toxins poisoning the environment prevented the growing of crops. With most of the stockpiled foodstuffs either having been eaten or hoarded by a few well-armed groups, a surprising number of survivors took to eating the only source of nutrition they could find: other people. Unfortunately, as had been demonstrated during the massive food riots in Third World countries in the years preceding the war, once established, cannibalism became addictive. Human flesh was the delicacy to top all delicacies.

For several minutes the hike eastward continued. The temperature dropped steadily, as it usually did after sunset in January, and a lively breeze only added to the chill factor.

"Glad I'm wearin' buckskins," Hickok commented.

Isabel Kaufer walked along in a subdued fashion, her posture stooped, her head bowed, detached from the world around her.

Studying the woman's profile, Blade wondered what was going through her mind. She'd heard their conversation, yet hadn't displayed any reaction. Given the comments Nathan had made, she should exhibit some concern for her safety. Had the death of her mate broken her spirit? Had she simply resigned herself to whatever Fate had in store?

More to the point, what *was* he going to do with her?

There were 32 members of the Resistance Movement seated in a semicircle in front of their leaders and the stranger, all listening attentively. Some were in chairs, most on the floor. All repeatedly glanced in wonder at the big man in the bizarre dark blue uniform bearing an ebony skull on the back.

Yama was aware of their interest. He stood with his arms crossed, listening to the top rebel, the man called Falcone, wrap up the strategy session.

"We'll succeed if every unit does its part," Falcone was saying. "Timing will be crucial. We'll have one hour to complete the sabotage from the time our new ally enters the Central Core."

One of the men raised a hand. "I don't mean to be critical, but how do we know we can trust this guy? He hasn't even told us his name yet."

The Warrior unfolded his arms. "I'm called Yama."

"An unusual name," remarked the white-haired freedom fighter, Roy, who was standing a few feet away.

"There is something else you should know," Yama stated. For the past hour he'd listened to them formulate their plans and been impressed by their efficiency. He'd learned that each of the people in the room was the head of a rebel cell comprised of 200 persons, on average, from all walks of life.

The Resistance Movement, as detailed by Falcone and Roy, had gained momentum daily. There were untold thousands who were morally sick of the status quo and eager to overthrow the established order. But concrete progress had been slow, positive results difficult to achieve, because the Technic elite were doing everything in their considerable power to eradicate the Movement in its infancy.

The fear the rebels inspired in the government had been demonstrated by the thousands of arrests made in recent months of anyone even remotely suspected of being connected to the Movement. Ironically, often the Technic Police Force arrested people who were innocent of any wrongdoing, but who had been anonymously turned in by someone with a grudge or by an enemy who'd seen a golden opportunity to eliminate a rival without repercussions.

Although the rebels were relatively poorly equipped and trained, they possessed a dynamic dedication that could prevail over insurmountable odds. All it would take would be the right spark to set the revolution ablaze, to have the cry of freedom spread like wildfire among the general populace.

All these thoughts ran through Yama's mind as he spoke. If the Spirit was willing, *he* would be the spark. After hearing the intimate details of Technic governmental administration from Roy, he'd devised a means of exploiting a weakness the Technic elite didn't realize existed. In fact, the government saw the weakness as a strength.

"What is it?" Falcone asked.

"I'm from the Home."

A ripple of excitement passed around the room.

"The same place as Hickok?" Falcone asked excitedly.

"The same," Yama confirmed.

"Everyone in the city knows of Hickok," Roy revealed. "He shook up the entire government when he killed the last Minister and broke out of the Central Core. The media played up the story for weeks. Frankly, I was surprised the government censors let them, until I realized the story was being used as propaganda to fuel hatred of your Family and the Freedom Federation."

Falcone nodded. "The government has done a fair job of brainwashing the average citizen into believing the Federation is out to annihilate every Technic."

"Yet none of you believe them," Yama noted.

"We don't believe anything those bastards try to sell us," Falcone said passionately. "All of us in the Movement have seen through their web of lies and deception. Most of us have had loved ones taken away by the sadistic police, never to be heard from again. We know from first-hand experience how truly monstrous our so-called leaders really are.''

''Death to the Minister!'' someone yelled.

''Down with the butchers!'' added another.

Roy smiled sheepishly at the man in blue. ''What we lack in expertise we more than make up in determination. Sooner or later the Movement will triumph. It's inevitable. Just like when the early American colonies were oppressed by England and when the countries of Eastern Europe were under the iron heel of Communism, the people of Technic City have been denied their freedom.'' He paused. ''Freedom is more than an inalienable right. It's a fundamental condition necessary for human happiness. No amount of government regulation and oppression can eliminate such a basic urge. Trying to suppress it is like trying to cap a volcano. Eventually that volcano will erupt and destroy those who tried to deny Nature.''

Falcone laughed lightly. ''You must forgive Roy, Yama. He's a political-science instructor at a university and tends to become long-winded. Maybe that's the reason they pay him such an exorbitant salary so he can afford this nice home.''

Some of the rebels chuckled.

''What do you do?'' the Warrior asked.

''I run a bookstore,'' Falcone said, and gestured at the seated rebels. ''Everyone here has a different occupation, but we're all united in our common cause.''

''Don't worry about them,'' Roy interjected. ''They'll do their part admirably.'' He looked into the big man's unnerving eyes. ''But what about you? Do you really think it can be done?''

''If I didn't, I wouldn't have proposed the idea,'' Yama

said. "Your rulers made a mistake when they placed all their eggs in one basket, so to speak. By concentrating all of their administrative agencies and military command centers in one edifice they centralized the government, but in the process they made that edifice their Achilles heel."

Falcone slowly shook his head. "I don't know," he said uncertainly. "If your plan works it'll be a miracle."

"Do any of you have a better idea?" Yama asked, and no one replied. "At the rate you've been going, it will be another ten or twenty years before your Movement even makes a dent. If I can succeed in creating chaos tomorrow, your units shouldn't encounter much opposition. Blowing up the military barracks and two-thirds of the police stations will drastically reduce the forces that can be thrown at you. And by taking over key communications facilities, you can broadcast your message of revolution to the entire city. From then on it will be up to the people. If they want freedom, they'll fight for it."

"And you?" Roy said. "What about you?"

"What about me?"

"You're committing suicide."

"Let me worry about that," Yama declared firmly, and looked at a clock on the wall. "It's now one A.M. Since we've already decided daylight would be too early and not give you time to get your units in place, at eight tomorrow morning I'll attack the Central Core."

CHAPTER
FIFTEEN

Falcone drove the trike himself, and delivered the Warrior to the west edge of the spacious parking lot surrounding the Central Core at ten minutes to eight. The magnificent structure sparkled in the bright morning sunshine. Since the typical workday for the majority of personnel employed at the Core began at seven A.M., the lot contained hundreds of trikes and four-wheelers as well as a few jeeps, trucks, and cars.

Yama wore a green trench coat to conceal his weapons. The Wilkinson and two Dakons were in a large red garment bag given to him by Roy. He had the bag draped across his thighs and one hand on Falcone's shoulder as the trike pulled up to the curb.

"End of the line," the rebel leader declared, looking over his shoulder.

Dismounting, Yama cradled the heavy bag in his left arm, and tugged at the wide-brimmed purple hat tendered by another member of the Movement to cover his distinctive hair and screen his face.

138 David Robbins

On the street beside them swarmed the usual heavy traffic.

"Let's synchronize watches," Falcone suggested. He wore an orange trench coat and a yellow polka-dot cap.

The warrior pulled back his left sleeve to expose the watch given to him by his newfound friend. A digital, and the very latest in Technic technology, it boasted 41 functions in addition to telling the time. Falcone had claimed the device could even monitor a person's blood pressure and pulse rate. "I have nine minutes until eight."

"Same here."

"Then we're all set," Yama said, hefting the garment bag.

"In more ways than one," Falcone stated. "My people are all in position. At eight sharp we begin."

"May the Spirit guide your every move."

Falcone twisted and gazed up at the tip of the glistening Core. "I don't see how you can possibly do it, and I don't understand why I believe you can."

"The Movement will have the hour it needs," Yama promised, and started to leave.

"Yama?"

"Yes?" the Warrior responded, pausing.

"Take care," Falcone said, and revved the engine. In seconds he'd blended into the traffic flow and was racing to the north.

Yama faced the edifice and walked across a narrow strip of grass to the lot. There were few people abroad, and none paid him the slightest attention. Threading a path among the parked vehicles, he soon came within 15 yards of the gold doors lining the Core's base.

There were two guards, soldiers with Dakon II's slung over their shoulders. They stood near the middle of the row of doors, conversing idly. Neither paid much attention to the Warrior until he was almost upon them. Then the shorter of the duo looked around in surprise and declared, "Hold it, citizen. Where do you think you're going?"

Yama casually unbuttoned the trench coat and halted six feet from them. "Sorry to bother you, but do you have the time?"

"Why don't you go find a phone and call Dial-the-Time?" the trooper suggested. "The number is 282-5000."

"Give him a break, Nick," said the other soldier, who checked his wristwatch. "It's three minutes till eight."

The Warrior eased his right hand under the trench coat. "Then I'll start early."

"Start what, citizen?" the short soldier asked, his brown eyes narrowing.

"Are either of you married?" Yama inquired.

Surprised by the unexpected query, the troopers looked at one another. The tall courteous one snickered and said, "No, citizen. Neither of us have tied the knot yet. Why do you want to know?"

"It's for the best," Yama said, and drew the Browning. A single shot bored a slug through the shorter man's brain, and the Technic spun and dropped. Yama shifted, aiming at the soldier who had given him the time, who was now gawking at him in horror.

"Don't," the man said.

"Drop your weapon and flee."

Stupefied by the order, the soldier nonetheless promptly let his Dakon slide to the cement walk and took off to the south. He never bothered to glance back.

Yama stared at the gold-plated doors for a moment, half expecting reinforcements to appear immediately. When none did, he placed the garment bag on the asphalt, crouched, and quickly unfastened the zipper. Shrugging out of the trench coat and tossing it aside, he replaced the Browning, slung the Wilkinson over his right arm, a Dakon II over his left, and gripped the second Dakon in both hands. His pockets bulged with ammo, clips, and magazines, and attached to his belt were six fragmentation grenades courtesy of the rebels. Rising, he strode up to the doors and spied a slender panel between two of them. As he'd been told would be the case, there were several buttons arranged vertically down the panel. He pressed one.

A door to his right hissed wide.

He went in swiftly and found an enormous, lavishly adorned lobby. There were three military men conversing off to the left, a pair of civilians straight ahead, and a counter along the right-hand wall manned by four people.

Everyone gaped at him as he entered.

Yama snapped the Dakon to his right shoulder and methodically squeezed off his shots, one bullet to a customer. The special dumdums fired by the rifle were amazing. Each round was programmed by a microchip to explode after penetrating several inches into any substance, whether flesh, wood, or metal.

He downed the three soldiers first, their heads bursting as if hit by buckshot and spraying brains, hair, and blood all over the thick red carpet.

The civilians started to run toward the row of elevators situated along the opposite wall.

Yama sent a dumdum into the back of each person's head, and swiveled toward the counter without wasting the time to verify they were dead. Two of the four at the counter had dropped from sight. The remaining pair, a man and a woman, stood with their mouths wide open, petrified by the slaughter. He sent a dumdum into the mouth of each.

Unexpectedly an alarm sounded, a strident blaring of klaxons.

He turned and walked to the elevators. Stabbing an up button, he kept his back to the wall while waiting for the car to open. It was well he did.

One of the gold doors slid to the left and in charged two police officers, service revolvers in their hands.

Yama slew both before they had an opportunity to spot him, drilling a dumdum into each man's chest. A bell went ping and the elevator arrived. He pivoted as the door opened, and discovered two army officers inside, both carrying briefcases. They were listening in concern to the klaxons. Their expressions changed to utter consternation when they beheld him.

"What the hell," one blurted out.

"Just possibly," Yama said, and leveled the Dakon. The rifle cracked twice, delivering a single round into each man's heart. They were thrown back against the rear of the car, and three-inch holes blossomed in their torsos as the miniature charges detonated. Crimson drops and bits of skin spattered on Yama's face.

He stepped into the car and hit the button for the ninth floor. On the tenth was the Minister's office and personal suite, his destination. But taking the elevator all the way up would be foolhardy. The rebels had advised him of a rumor that the top of the shaft had been wired with explosives so the Minister, with the flick of a switch, could reduce the car and any hostile occupants to miniscule pieces when the elevator arrived on the upper floor.

Yama watched the indicator lights on the inner panel as the car climbed steadily. He passed the second, third, and fourth. On every floor the klaxons were shrieking.

Suddenly, as the car came to the fifth floor, it halted and the door opened.

Framed in the corridor were six soldiers, each armed with a Dakon II, evidently on their way downstairs, where they believed the intruder to be. They took one look at the big man in blue and tried to bring their weapons into play.

Yama was faster. A slight motion of his right thumb switched the Dakon's selector lever from single to full auto, and his fingers stroked the trigger. In the confines of the elevator the blasting of the Dakon was deafening.

All six troopers took the lethal hail of dumdums straight on, their bodies dancing and jerking as they were riddled. Behind them arose shouts and the pounding of others coming to their aid.

The instant the magazine went empty Yama punched the control panel, and the door closed and the elevator resumed its ascent. He pressed the release button on the rifle, extracted the spent magazine, and pulled a fresh one from a back pocket. The rebels had supplied him with enough ammo to wage World War Four, and he intended to avail himself of every round.

The car passed the sixth and seventh floors.

Yama detached a grenade from his belt, his eyes on the indicators. He hoped to reach the ninth without difficulty, but the car again whined to a stop on the eighth. His finger slid into the grenade's pin, and he was about to pull it when the door folded inward to reveal a startled woman in a white laboratory smock standing there with a yellow notebook in her left hand.

She screamed.

He stepped from the car, curled his hand around the pineapple, and clipped her on the jaw with it.

The woman's teeth crunched together and blood spurted from her mouth. She staggered rearward a few feet and collapsed.

Beyond her was a long white corridor with dozens of doors on each side. Frozen in the act of going somewhere or other were a score of men and women similarly attired in white smocks.

Some kind of scientific research department, Yama reasoned. He wagged the Dakon at the people in the hall and they all scattered, darting or diving through doorways. In seconds the corridor was empty. He started to turn toward the elevator.

With another ping the door abruptly closed.

Annoyed at himself for not acting sooner, Yama saw the arrow overhead drop rapidly toward the first floor. He glanced down the corridor, wary of being shot in the back, and spied an EXIT sign halfway down.

Just what he needed.

Yama rotated and raced toward the exit, going by door after door, most slamming shut a few steps before he reached them. Those still open afforded access to unoccupied chambers. In some he saw long tables bearing various beakers and racks of vials. Other rooms contained electronic equipment.

All the time the klaxons wailed on.

He had a good dozen yards still to cover when a bearded man in an immaculate smock stepped from a room up ahead and pointed a peculiar device at him. The object consisted of a silver rod jutting from the center of a small black box. At the end of the rod was a small golden ball or globe. Not knowing what it was and unwilling to find out the hard way, he dived onto his stomach, firing in midair.

The scientist had just squeezed the trigger on the box when a neat pattern of red holes stitched across the front of the smock and he was flung onto his back, the device flying from his limp fingers.

Yama saw a thin red beam of light shoot from the gold ball even as the man fell, and heard a sizzling sound as it shot over his head. As quickly as the light appeared, it vanished. He rose and ran to the still, bleeding scientist. Slipping the grenade into a front pocket, he picked up the device. What in the world could it be? He'd never heard of such a bizarre weapon.

There were only two buttons on the black box. One was marked FIRE, the other RECHARGE.

Intriguing but useless, Yama decided, and tossed the unique weapon to the floor. He hastened onward. For his plan to succeed, for him to keep every administrator and military official in the Central Core preoccupied for the better part of an hour, he must reach the Minister.

The EXIT door was unlocked, and he moved through it onto a wide landing. Gazing over the railing he saw the bottom far below. From down there came yelling and the clumping of heavy boots.

Yama went up, taking the steps three at a stride. He reached the ninth floor landing and halted, recalling the intelligence information relayed by the rebels. On this floor were stationed 20 or 30 seasoned troops, the Minister's personal guard unit. He went to the door, twisted the knob slowly, and opened it a crack.

Sure enough, there were several dozen soldiers congregated near the elevator shaft, spread out so four or five troopers covered each one. An officer stood to one side, issuing instructions.

Removing the genade from his pocket, Yama set the Dakon down and pulled the pin. Holding the safety lever flush with the serrated body, he tugged the door wider, took a stride, and heaved.

Someone spotted him and shouted a warning.

Yama whirled and darted onto the landing, pressing the door closed with one hand as he scooped up the Dakon II with the other. He flattened a heartbeat before one or more of the troopers blistered the door at chest height.

With a loud whomp! the grenade went off.

That should delay them a bit, Yama reflected, shoving upright. He took several steps, making for the tenth floor, but he'd only covered half the landing when he saw the huge creature bounding down the stairwell toward him and he drew up short in amazement.

The thing was a dog.

CHAPTER
SIXTEEN

The Warriors of Alpha Triad and their captive had covered
five miles by eight in the morning. Hickok took point,
strolling along as if he didn't have a care in the world,
ten yards ahead of Blade and Geronimo, who were
walking side by side and discussing the fate of Isabel
Kauler.

"Why don't we just let her go?" Geronimo suggested,
keeping his voice down so she couldn't hear him.

Blade glanced over his right shoulder at the woman,
who trailed ten feet behind. Let her go? He'd like to, but
he felt oddly responsible for her welfare. Her dejected
posture hadn't improved any since the night before; if
anything, it had worsened. She hadn't made any attempt
to escape, which puzzled him. Perhaps it was because she
had to squint against the light and tears were constantly
in her eyes. "Hickok thinks we should kill her," Blade
mentioned. "He's even volunteered to do the job."

"Nice guy."

"I can see his point," Blade said. "She's too dangerous

to let go. She might kill someone, might eat them, and we would indirectly be responsible because we had the chance to eliminate her and didn't.''

"Eliminate her," Geronimo repeated distastefully. "You make it sound so clinical, like you're performing a surgical operation.''

"In a sense it is.''

"Maybe so, but there is something else we could try.''

"What?" Blade asked.

"We could try to change her,'' Geronimo proposed in all earnestness.

"Rehabilitate a cannibal?" Blade said skeptically. "I don't know if it's ever been done.''

"Is that any reason not to try? We could take her to the Home, let the Elders decide,'' Geronimo said. He added wistfully, "If they vote for execution, then Hickok or Ares or Lynx will be more than willing to handle the chore and not have a qualm doing it.''

"You sound jealous.''

"I am,'' Geronimo freely admitted. "Nathan and a few of the others can terminate anyone without a twinge of conscience. Me, I'm different. I'll kill in the line of duty, but there are times when I'm lying in bed at night that I'll see the faces of those I've slain in my mind's eye. It bothers me a little.''

"We all go through the same thing at one time or another,'' Blade said. He pondered his friend's idea. At first thought it was patently ridiculous, but the more he debated the pros and cons the more it appealed to him. He had reservations, though, about taking Isabel to the Home. What if she harmed a Family member? There were dozens of young children there, including his own son Gabe.

Perhaps the issue boiled down to one thing: Did the woman deserve a second chance? The answer had to be

yes, but only if *she* wanted to change. And as far as the
Family was concerned, they'd shown a remarkable,
commendable adaptability to admitting new members,
even when those seeking permission to live at the Home
were potentially dangerous. After all, Lynx had been a
genetically engineered assassin created by the vile Doktor,
a man who'd tried to destroy the Home and wipe out the
Family, yet the cat-man had been welcomed and accepted
with open arms.

"How do you deal with it?" Geronimo inquired.

Engrossed in reflection, Blade barely heard the
question. He blinked and looked at him. "What?"

"How do you deal with the ghosts of those you've
slain?" Geronimo elaborated.

"I try not to dwell on them," Blade replied. "We're
Warriors. Killing is just part of our job, a grisly part that
has often meant the difference between life and death for
each of us and the Family. You have to put it behind you,
file it in a part of your brain where it'll remain buried,
or the memories will eat at you and ruin your ability to
get the job done right."

"Easier said then done."

Blade saw Hickok suddenly glance at them, wheel, and
hurry back. "Did you see something?" he asked.

"I sure did, pard," the gunfighter responded, and
smirked.

"What's so funny?" Geronimo wondered.

"You two clowns."

"Meaning what?"

Hickok chuckled. "Meaning that while the two of you
were gabbin' like hens the cannibal flew the coop."

Startled, Blade spun.

Sure enough, Isabel Kauler was gone.

At eight A.M. the first explosions rocked Technic City.

Four barracks housing several hundred soldiers were destroyed simultaneously, followed seconds later by ten strategic police stations that were scattered about the city.

The Technic Broadcasting Station, situated in a seven-story skyscraper a mile north of the Central Core, was going about its daily routine when dozens of blue-garbed rebels poured into the lobby, overwhelming the meager force of security guards without firing a shot.

Falcone led this detachment personally. While fifteen rebels remained downstairs, the rest took control of one floor after another. The stunned broadcasters and journalists offered no resistance.

Beaming out over the metropolis from Studio Five was the popular *Exercise with Marsha* show. Seductive, rapier-thin Marsha and her four leotard-clad assistants were demonstrating how to do tummy tucks when in burst the Resistance Movement. They froze in the act of tucking.

Falcone marched over to the camera, pointed his Dakon II at the operator, and declared, "Keep it on me or else."

"Yes, sir," the shocked cameraman said.

"People of Technic City," Falcone began, having memorized every word of the speech the night before, "I'm the leader of the Resistance Movement. At this very moment the revolt against tyranny for which you have long waited is in full swing. We now control the television station. The army and police forces are in disarray. There will never be another chance like this again.

"If you have longed to know true freedom, if you're fed up with the government, with the Technic elite dictating every aspect of our lives, then you should join us. We desperately need your support. With your help we can establish a new, democratic government in our fair city. With your help we can create a brand new future.

"Listen out the window of your home or business. Listen wherever you are. Those explosions and the gunfire you hear are the chimes of liberty for all of us. Join us in overthrowing the dictators who oppress us at every turn.

"Those who want freedom must fight for it. If you, like I, value freedom as the most precious gift our Creator has bestowed on us, then prove your devotion by joining our cause.

"Our government has become a model of tyranny because we have let it. We are taxed to the breaking point, our property subject to confiscation without due process, our children taken from us and raised by unfeeling government drones. The government presumes to tell us how we must live, to dictate every aspect of our lives from the food we eat to the clothes we wear. They even go so far as to tell us how we must *think*.

"Enough is enough! It is time to throw off the yoke of civil slavery! Rally around us! Flock to your banner, and by this time tomorrow Technic City will belong to the people again. We can form a new government, a government of the people, for the people, and by the people."

Falcone stopped, flushed with enthusiasm, and held his right fist aloft in a symbolic gesture of hopeful victory. "Stay tuned for more details," he added, and turned toward the host of *Exercise with Marsha*. "You may continue for the time being."

"Thank you."

Several rebels had already taken over the control booth, and Falcone now hurried up a short flight of stairs and joined them. "Has there been any reaction from the Central Core?"

A woman pointed at a special red telephone on the wall. "No, sir. Not a peep. I doubt they know we've taken over the building yet."

"Good. Yama was right. The government made a blunder when it put all of its eggs in one basket. Permitting only a single TV station to exist will prove their undoing.''

A man came running in. ''Falcone, we've started broadcasting on all radio channels. Roy is using the tapes he
made.''

''Okay. Tell him to stay there until further notice.''

''Yes, sir.'' The man whirled and dashed off.

Falcone smiled encouragement at the rebels in the
booth. ''So far, so good. If the rest of the units do their
job equally as well, we'll prevail.''

One of the freedom fighters stepped to a window and
opened it. The sharp sounds of automatic weapon fire
mingled with louder detonations. There were screams and
shouts and terrified wails.

''It sounds like the end of the world,'' commented an
awed rebel.

''Yes, doesn't it?'' Falcone said, and beamed.

The switchboard operators at the Central Core were
doing the best they could, but the madhouse within and
the bedlam without made their job impossible. Scores of
calls came in from frantic police, military officers, and
politicians requesting assistance or instructions. But the
operators were unable to connect the calling parties with
their administrative heads or superior officers because
none were in their offices.

The majority of workers in the Central Core, from
secretaries to high-ranking commanders, had joined the
general exodus from the building after the alarm was
sounded and a rumor spread that a rebel suicide squad
had attacked the Core and planned to blow it up.

One man, however, adamantly refused to leave. He
stood at a window, observing the dozens of columns of
gray and black smoke arising from his city, seeing crowds
of rampaging citizens in the streets far below, and listening
to the muffled popping of firearms. A powerful explosion

not two blocks away shook the pane as another police station went up in flames.

Ramis ran up and said crisply, "Except for your personal guard, everyone else on the ninth floor has gone down in the elevators, sir."

The Minister turned. "You weren't able to stop them?"

"No, sir. General Schonfeld gave the order several minutes ago. I was too late."

"It wasn't your fault," the Minister stated. "Where is that incompetent Schonfeld now?"

"Still on the ninth floor. As I was talking to him there was a blast in the background and the line went dead."

"Go inform him in person that I want to see him."

"And if he won't come?"

The Minister's features hardened darkly. "Then he'll face a court-martial after we've taught the rebels the folly of opposing their betters. Now go."

"Yes, sir," Ramis said dutifully, and hastened away.

Scowling, the Minister gazed out the window again. To the west a small group of soldiers were advancing in formation toward the Core. Suddenly, from out of every alley and side street in their vicinity poured a hoard of screeching citizens armed with baseball bats, rolling pins, kitchen knives, and anything else that had been handy. The soldiers halted and brought their Dakons to bear with practiced precision, mowing down the foremost ranks of the howling mob. But the human wave couldn't be halted by a few lead pebbles; it crashed into the troopers and engulfed them in a savage swirl of bloody fighting. Half a minute later not a soldier remained alive.

Pivoting, the Minister walked to a console on the left-hand wall and pressed a button. Instantly a television screen came to life above him, but instead of an approved program he saw an unfamiliar man in a blue rebel uniform exhorting the populace to rush from their homes and join the growing revolution.

Furious, the Minister smashed his fist down on the button and the screen went blank.

Behind him someone nervously cleared his throat.

Pivoting, the Minister regarded the four scientists in their white smocks and the pair of Cy-Hounds held on a tight leash by two of them. He walked over, his face a tingle of crimson. "Did you see? Did you hear? Those rabble think they can defeat me! I'll have every one of them tortured before they die."

"Yes, sir," the senior biochemical engineer replied. "They certainly deserve such a punishment."

"They deserve far worse," the Minister hissed, and focused on the Cy-Hounds. "Why hasn't the third one returned yet?"

"I don't know," said the senior scientist.

"You assured me that it would find the intruders and terminate them. Yet it's been five minutes since you sent it out the door."

The man swallowed. "Begging your pardon, Excellency, but the Central Core is an enormous structure. There's no telling on which floor the rebels might be. But you can rest assured that the Cy-Hound will find them. Its brain is actually a marvelous computer enabling it to identify criminal types not only by their behavior, but by their clothing, scent, heart rate, and other programmed factors. The Cy-Hound reacts to the composite total."

"Elaborate."

"Let's say the Cy-Hound comes across a civilian holding a weapon. Since it's programmed to know that only men and women dressed in proper police or military uniforms are permitted to carry a firearm, it will automatically attack."

"Let's hope these beasts are all you claim they are," the Minister said gruffly. "If not, we might very well have rebels coming in that door."

"Not to worry, sir," the scientist stated confidently. "We still have this pair. If rebels come through that door, the Cy-Hounds will tear them to pieces."

CHAPTER SEVENTEEN

The thing was a dog.

Or was it?

Yama leveled the Dakon II as the creature halted abruptly on the steps above, its smooth, gray, hairless body rippling with distinctive sinews. He'd never encountered a beast quite like it, and wondered if it might be a mutation.

Five feet high at the shoulders, the strange canine possessed a massive build and appeared to weigh close to two hundred pounds. The legs were short and stout, the body shaped like a barrel. Its face had a square profile. The nose was black, the lips thin. Most startling were the eyes. They contained bizarre reddish pupils that had the transparency of clear plastic and glowed with a fiery inner light. Around its thick neck hung a wide black leather collar bearing inch-long silver studs.

The Warrior hoped the thing would keep on going. At any moment he expected irate soldiers to come piling through the door, and he didn't care to be trapped between them and the dog.

Shouts arose in the corridor attended by the sound of troopers rushing toward the stairwell.

The strange brute cocked its head and sniffed loudly.

Yama went into action, removing another grenade and pulling the pin as he backpedaled to the door, keeping his eyes on the beast. He opened the door a foot and saw a dozen troopers charging straight at him. Quickly he hurled the grenade and slammed the door before they could open up, moving to the right as he did.

From his rear came the faint scratching of claws on the floor.

Spinning, Yama tried to bring the Dakon into play.

Its lips curled back to expose thin, razor-edge teeth, the brute was already on the attack, springing toward the big man in blue. Oddly, the dog didn't growl or snarl or bark. It simply closed for the kill with all the cold precision of a ruthless machine.

Yama had the Dakon in front of his chest when the canine leaped and slammed into him, grabbing the barrel in its massive jaws and chomping down at the moment of impact. The force of the heavy body knocked Yama against the wall at the same instant the grenade detonated. He felt the wall vibrate and the floor trembled slightly, and then he forgot all about the Technic troopers as he fought for his life against the beast.

Landing on all fours, the dog retained its grip on the barrel and jerked his head to the left.

The Warrior would never have believed such a feat possible, but the animal tore the Dakon from his grasp. He darted to the left, striving to put a little distance between them and buy time to bring another gun into play.

Dropping the Dakon, the canine lowered its head and vaulted at its intended victim.

Yama couldn't evade the rush. He didn't bother to try. Instead, he went with the flow of the creature's attack, employing a basic judo and jujitsu techique of using an adversary's momentum against him. His hands flicked out and grasped the dog's extended front legs, and as his fingers closed on its cold skin he dropped his right shoulder and pivoted, whipping the animal into the wall.

Letting go, Yama glided to the center of the landing and tried to unsling the other Dakon. The dog scrambled erect and came at him again, forcing him to give up on the rifle and go for his scimitar. His right arm was a blur as he drew and slashed.

The edge of the scimitar caught the canine at the base of its throat and slit it from one side to the other. Twisting, the animal shifted to the right and paused.

Yama held the scimitar ready for a second swing, his eyes glued to the thing's neck, waiting for its blood to gush forth. But no blood seeped out. He was certain the blade had cut a half-inch deep, yet there was no blood. How could that be?

Dodging first one way, then the other, the gray brute snapped at the Warrior's legs.

Retreating, Yama swung and missed several times in succession. The creature's reflexes were incredible. Yama couldn't score no matter how hard he tried. Another swipe drove the beast back a yard, and Yama went for his Magnum, clearing leather with a speed that would have done justice to Hickok. He snapped off two shots, the retorts booming eerily in the stairwell, planting each directly between the canine's eyes.

Staggered by the impact, the brute staggered rearward, its knees beginning to buckle. Exhibiting astonishing strength, the dog recovered, straightened, and shook its head a few times. Where any other dog would have been dead on the spot, this one exposed its fangs and renewed its assault.

Bewildered for one of the few times in his life, Yama

kept the beast at bay with the scimitar and backed toward the stairs leading up to the tenth floor. He realized the thing couldn't be a mutation because even mutants bled. What in the world was it then? A creation of the Technics? If so, what kind? What weak spots did it have? A grenade would do the job, but he had to get far enough away to escape the blast himself before he could use one.

Or did he?

An insane idea occurred to him and he holstered the Magnum. His left foot bumped into the bottom step. He halted, formulating his strategy. When the beast darted forward, he countered with a wide downward strike that missed but drove the thing over four feet to the rear. In a flash he transferred the scimitar to his left hand and pulled a grenade. He had to use his thumb to extract the pin one-handed.

The brute crouched, its feral eyes blazing, its muscles coiling like springs, and suddenly sprang.

Yama was ready. He dropped the scimitar and stepped in closer, meeting the dog midway, twisting his body so that those wicked teeth missed his chest and clamping his left arm around the beast's neck as he did the unthinkable and drove his right fist, curled around the grenade, into its open mouth.

The creature tried to bite his arm off.

Lancing pain racked Yama's arm as he crammed the grenade down its throat and wrenched his arm out again. The dog's teeth dug in deep, shredding his sleeve and cutting furrows in his flesh. As his hand slid free the beast's jaws snapped shut, almost taking off several fingers.

Thrashing, the brute tried to break loose of the big man's grasp.

Yama looped his injured arm around its neck and surged toward the railing, ticking off the seconds in his mind.

Fragmentation grenades had a four- to five-second time delay between the release of the safety lever and detonation of the six and a half ounces of explosive inside. By his count, three of those seconds were expended when he reached the railing and heaved the struggling, snapping canine over.

He dropped the creature and whirled. Taking one long stride, he launched himself into the air and struck the landing just as the frag went off. The landing shook under him.

Bits and pieces of the canine rained down. Sections of skin, parts of metallic bones, and chunks of fleshlike substance pelted the Warrior and spattered all around him.

Yama couldn't stay idle. Swiftly he retrieved the scimitar and the Dakon, but when he picked up the latter he discovered the dog's teeth had cracked the barrel and rendered the weapon useless. He unslung the second Dakon, worked the cocking handle, and stepped to the door and opened it.

Littering the hallway were a couple of dozen injured or dead troopers. Many groaned or clutched their sides and cried pitiably. There was no one else around.

Where had the rest gone? Yama asked himself, and turned from the ninth floor to begin his ascent to the tenth and final level on which he would find the Minister. Blood dripped from his right forearm and trickled onto the Dakon, making his grip slippery. He halted and used the survival knife to slice off several wide strips from his left sleeve for makeshift bandages. Wrapping them around the deep cuts, he tightened the strips as best he could with his teeth and left hand, then tied large knots to hold the bandages in place.

Satisfied with his handiwork, Yama climbed higher. He slowed as he neared the last landing, anticipating there would be guards. None were stationed there, however, and he came to a closed door without further mishap.

He slowly twisted the knob and gently pulled until he could see the large chamber within. The sight of another pair of nasty creatures similar to the persistent dog he'd dispatched brought a frown to his mouth. There were also four scientists in white smocks and one other person, a thin man with oily blond hair who wore a uniform that perfectly contrasted with Yama's outfit: light, bright blue, and adorned with gold trim.

That must be the Minister, Yama decided, about to fling the door wide and barge in when he noticed the dogs again. Both of the nearly indestructible hounds were looking in his direction. They'd seen or heard him!

A white-haired scientist said something to the Minister, who looked at the door and smiled.

"Don't be shy," the Lord of Technic City stated in a mocking tone. "Whoever you are, enter."

Yama did so. He cradled the Dakon II and stopped just inside the doorway, scanning the chamber for other parties. Neither of the canines budged; their collars were attached to leashes held by a pair of the men in the white smocks.

The Minister stepped a few feet nearer, his countenance serene, completely unruffled. "So, it isn't a rebel suicide squad after all. I should have suspected as much."

Angling the rifle at the brutes, Yama walked to within a yard of the man he had traveled eight hundred miles to topple.

"You must be the one Corporal Carson told us about, the Warrior named Yama," the Minister said, studying the big man from head to toe.

"I am," Yama confirmed, watching the beasts. He felt confident the Dakon would slay both should they attack. The scientists barely deserved notice; they were no threat whatsoever.

"Fascinating," the Minister stated. "And what do you propose to do now?"

"Hold you hostage until the appointed time."

"Me? A hostage? How quaint." The Minister pressed his hands together and laughed, genuinely delighted.

From beyond the tinted windows came the sounds of a city at war: crackling gunfire, explosions, screams, and cries.

The Minister nodded toward the windows. "I take it that is your doing?"

"More or less."

Shaking his head and clucking, the Minister walked over to a chair and casually took a seat. "I should thank you."

"Why?"

"Because I've learned an important lesson today. I've learned never to underestimate the influence a single person can have. When that idiotic corporal informed me that a lone Warrior had come here to destroy our fair city, I almost laughed in his face. I was certain you must be insane."

"You were wrong," Yama declared.

"So I see," the Minister said. He sighed and glanced at the dogs, then at the Warrior. "There's an aspect to this affair I don't understand, and perhaps you would consent to providing an explanation?"

Yama simply waited.

"You allegedly told the corporal that you were doing this for Lieutenant Alicia Farrow. I ran a records check and learned Farrow had been sent to the Home about two years ago. She was supposed to aid a demolition team in gaining entry so your accursed compound could be destroyed. Something went wrong, though. Nothing was ever heard from Farrow or the team again," the Minister said, and made a tent of his fingers in his lap. "Tell me.

How does she fit into the scheme of things where you're concerned?''

"We were in love. She sacrificed herself to save me from the demolition team.''

The Minister scrutinized the Warrior's face. "Incredible. So all this is because you blame the Technics for her death?''

"I blame the system, not the people. For a century the Technic political and educational systems have produced the equivalent of robots, virtual slaves who don't even know the definition of true freedom. The citizens have regarded the government here as benevolent and concerned with the welfare of the common people, when we both know that governments are only interested in perpetuating more and stricter controls over those being ruled.''

"You're not at all what I expected,'' the Minister said. "Here I thought you were a muscle-bound oaf, when you actually possess a keen mind.''

Yama wasn't about to thank the man for the compliment. He aligned his finger snug with the trigger and listened to the warfare in the streets.

"It's most interesting that you should bring up the subject of robots,'' the Minister commented.

"Why?''

The Minister indicated the beasts with a curt nod. "Do you know what they are?''

"Dogs, but different from any dogs I've ever known.''

"In more ways than you realize,'' the Minister said, and chuckled. "Those exceptional creatures are biomechanical constructs, Cy-Hounds we call them.''

"I met one a few minutes ago,'' Yama disclosed. "They're not very friendly.''

The Minister glanced at the Warrior. "What happened to it, if I may ask?''

"It developed a bad case of indigestion."

"You must be a remarkable man to have defeated a Cy-Hound all by yourself," the Minister said. "And I can't help but wonder if you can do equally as well against two." He suddenly jabbed his finger at the beasts. "Release them."

Yama crouched, his finger tightening, but the pair of fierce Cy-Hounds were already in rapid motion, their rapier-lined mouths opened wide to tear into his body.

CHAPTER
EIGHTEEN

"Beats me why you're so ticked off, pard," Hickok commented, grinning. "This way you don't have to worry about whether we should blow her brains out or give her a spankin'."

Blade halted and glared at the gunfighter. The three of them had been in pursuit of Isabel Kaufer for ten minutes and not yet overtaken her. Geronimo, in the lead, was on one knee examining the ground; if anyone could find her, it would be him. When it came to tracking Geronimo had few equals.

"Why are you lookin' at me like that?" Hickok asked the peeved giant. "I figured you'd be tickled pink that she vamoosed."

"Sometimes, Nathan. Sometimes," Blade said, and faced Geronimo. "How far behind her are we?"

"Wait a blamed second!" Hickok interjected. "Sometimes what? You didn't finish."

"Yes, I did," Blade said.

"Bull patties. You can't just say 'sometimes' to

someone and let it go at that. What the blazes did it mean?''

''It meant that sometimes you can be a royal pain in the butt.''

''Oh. Was that all?''

Straightening, Geronimo pointed to the northwest. ''My guess would be she's heading home, back to that house, and making good time. We're about three or four minutes behind her.''

''Then if we push it we should catch her easily,'' Blade stated.

Geronimo looked at him. ''Are you sure you want to catch her?''

''Don't you start. Head on out.''

''Okay.''

The Warriors moved swiftly through the forest, covering hundreds of yards in three times the speed of an average person. They came to a gurgling, shallow stream and halted on the small bank.

Squatting, Geronimo indicated hand prints in the soft mud at the water's edge. ''She knelt here to get a drink.''

''I wouldn't mind wettin' my own whistle,'' Hickok remarked, and started to bend down.

Abruptly shattering the tranquility of the woodland, a terrified scream arose on the other side of the stream, coming from a dense stand of saplings.

''That was her!'' Geronimo exclaimed.

Blade sprinted to her rescue, splashing through the ankle-high water and vaulting onto the opposite bank. He grasped the Commando securely and plunged into the stand, threading between the slender young trees. A feral growling and snarling guided his footsteps to Kauler and a monstrosity straight out of a madman's nightmare, a mutation spawned by the radiation and chemical toxins polluting the land.

The woman had clambered up a ten-foot-high sapling, and was clinging for dear life near the top. Her weight bent the tree, and her legs were within inches of the slavering genetic deviate trying to eat her.

Stopping, Blade raised the Commando and tried to get a bead on the thing.

Perhaps the animal's ancestors had been common weasels. In its general shape the mutant resembled such small carnivores. But this specimen reared nearly seven feet high on its short hind legs, and had a thick but sinuous body a yard in circumference. Isolated tufts of brownish fur dotted its dark, leathery hide like weeds jutting from a parched plain. A scruffy tail a yard long jerked spasmodically as the mutant weaved this way and that, its green eyes fixed on its intended meal. Large yellow claws on all four feet appeared capable of ripping any prey to shreds. A small, rounded head perched on a long, thin neck gave the weasel a snakelike aspect. As it tried to tear the woman from the tree, snarls and hisses issued from its mouth, revealing scores of tiny daggers for teeth.

Try as Blade might, he couldn't keep the thing's head in his sights for more than a second at a time. The mutation kept moving, its head bobbing and darting right and left. He didn't want to fire until he was certain he could slay it, so he held his fire and heard his friends race up beside him.

Isabel spotted them and wailed, "Help me, please!"

Displaying exceptional intelligence, the weasel saw her looking to the southeast and did the same. The very instant that its eyes alighted on the Warriors it charged.

Blade fired, holding the barrel low to avoid accidentally hitting Isabel. At a range of only ten yards he could hardly miss. Or so he thought.

With the speed of a striking cobra, the weasel flashed

across the ground, winding from side to side like a rattler. A dozen rounds came close to its streaking form, chewing up the grass and sending clumps of turf flying. None scored a hit, though.

Hickok entered the fray, his Colts sweeping up and out and cracking twice apiece.

The weasel shuddered as the slugs tore into its body, but it never slowed.

Too late Blade realized he was its target, and he had barely braced his legs when the mutation plowed into his chest and bowled him over. He released the Commando as he fell and slammed onto his back with the ravenous horror on top of him. Its teeth snapped at his face, but he managed to get his left hand on its neck, under its jaw, and held its fetid mouth mere inches from his nose. Claws dug into his chest and legs. His right hand arced down and grasped the hilt of his Bowie, and on the upswing he buried the keen blade in the weasel's heaving side.

As quick as lightning the mutation wrenched loose and darted to the right, crouching for another attack, blood pouring from the wound.

Shots blasted, Hickok's Colts and Geronimo's FNC combining in a thunderous chorus, both men moving toward the mutant as they fired.

Caught in a hailstorm of burning slugs, the weasel went down. Immediately it surged upright and tried to flee, darting toward a thicket, snarling at the Warriors all the while. More rounds bored through its body and it sprawled onto its stomach.

Blade rose at the moment the Pythons and the FNC went empty. He took two strides and leaped, landing on the mutant's back as it heaved onto all fours. Wrapping his left arm around its neck, he stabbed the Bowie again and again into the deviate's body.

The weasel became a whirlwind, spinning and rolling and thrashing in a frenzied effort to dislodge the man-thing causing it so much agony.

His prodigious muscles bulging, Blade held on with all his might and continued stabbing, stabbing, stabbing. He glimpsed the thicket near at hand, and then the mutation stumbled again, tottered a few feet, and collapsed, its legs outflung, to hiss out a last, lingering breath.

In the heavy silence that ensued, Blade could hear his own heart thumping. The front of his body ached terrible. He uncoiled his left arm and sat up, staring at the weasel's glazing eyes.

Hickok and Geronimo came over, the former in the act of reloading his prized Pythons.

"That looked like fun," the gunfighter said. "You'd be a whiz at bronc-bustin'."

"No thanks," Blade said, looking down at the lacerations made by the mutant's claws. They were bleeding but superficial.

Geronimo stood over the weasel. "This is a new type. It amazes me how many different varieties of mutations we encounter on our travels."

"I don't mind bumpin' into them," Hickok said. "It's the fact they're always tryin' to eat me that gets my goat."

"Isabel is lucky we arrived when we did," Geronimo remarked.

At the mention of the woman's name all three Warriors turned toward the tree in which she'd roosted to find her gone.

"Blast!" Hickok declared. "Where did she mosey off to now?"

Blade stood. "Geronimo, find her tracks."

"Here we go again," the Blackfoot said, moving to the base of the tree.

Wiping the Bowie clean on his pants, Blade retrieved the Commando. He slid the knife into its sheath.

"Are we going after her?" Hickok inquired.

"Of course."

"Why bother, pard? Why not let her leave if she wants? It's no skin off our noses if a critter decides to have her for a snack."

"Like it or not, we're responsible for her," Blade said, walking over to the tree. "We brought her all this way."

Bent at the waist, Geronimo was inspecting the ground carefully. "That mutation really tore up the soil. It's hard to distinguish her prints with all the claw marks." He leaned down farther and grinned. "Here's a complete track. From the way the toes are aligned, I'd say she's still bearing to the northwest."

"Still trying to get home," Blade said thoughtfully. He hiked onward, taking the lead. "She can't be far ahead of us. It shouldn't take us very long to catch her."

The assessment proved to be inaccurate.

For five minutes the Warriors pursued the cannibal. The forest thinned and they reached a wide meadow where a herd of grazing deer was spooked by their arrival and bounded into the trees. Beyond the meadow rose a boulder-strewn hill. Nowhere did they spot any sign of Kauler.

"That woman must have wings on her feet," Hickok quipped.

In single file they jogged across the meadow to the base of the hill.

"Here are some more of her tracks," Geronimo announced, jabbing a finger at a set of three partial footprints in the soil. "She went straight up."

Hickok shook his head and chuckled. "Where does she get all her energy?"

"It's all the protein in her diet," Geronimo joked, and they both laughed.

"Not funny," Blade informed them, starting toward the summit. Scores of boulders obstructed his view of the top. He wound among them, his legs pumping, confident he would catch her soon because he doubted anyone could long maintain the pace she had so far.

Above him there came a loud thump and a crackling noise.

Blade glanced higher, and froze in shock at seeing a large boulder rolling down the slope toward them. "Take cover," he shouted, and glanced right and left, spotting an even bigger boulder he could use as a shelter.

The five-ton projectile rapidly gained momentum, flattening brush in its path and bouncing off other boulders, but hurtling on a relatively straight course.

Dashing behind the boulder he'd selected, Blade grinned at his companions and saw them similarly taking cover. Then the rockly cannonball rumbled past his sanctuary and kept on going, careening off another boulder on its way to the bottom of the hill. When it hit, the entire hill seemed to quake and a dust cloud swirled into the cool air.

Hickok stepped from concealment. "A few more seconds and we would have known what it feels like to be a flapjack."

"Was that an accident?" Geronimo inquired, stepping out.

Blade speculated on the same question. He rounded the boulder and scanned the slope above, but saw no one. Still uneasy, he climbed as fast as he could.

"Wait for us, pard," Hickok urged.

Motioning for them to hurry, Blade ascended to the spot where he'd first beheld the large boulder, and went an additional five yards. There he found what he'd suspected he would: a barren circular depression on the rim of an earthen knob and beside it a long, sturdy, straight limb. He deduced the boulder had been precariously balanced, and the woman had used the limb to rock it loose and send it clattering downward.

What was that?

Blade tensed, hearing a peculiar sound, a soft, fluttering whine. He hustled even higher, the whine becoming louder, until he saw her.

Isabel Kauler was on hands and knees, breathing in exhausted, ragged gasps, her fingers digging into the earth as she desperately tried to claw her way to the summit. When a huge shadow fell across her she recoiled in stark fear and curled into a fetal position, crying hysterically.

Blade gazed down at her, his emotions in turmoil. His fellow Warriors joined him and neither spoke a word.

Cringing and hiding her face with her hands, the woman trembled violently.

"Isabel?" Blade said softly.

"No!" she screeched. "Don't hurt me! Please don't hurt me! Let me go!"

The unadulterated, almost palpable fear in her voice brought goose bumps to Blade's skin. "Isabel, please," he said, and squatted to touch her on the shoulder.

Shrieking, Isabel reacted as if touched by the hand of death. She tried to scramble rearward, but bumped into a boulder. "Don't kill me! I don't want to die!" she pleaded, tears gushing down her cheeks.

Blade glanced at his friends, noting their somber expressions, and bowed his head.

Isabel cried for several minutes, sniffling and mewing like a lost kitten. Gradually her hysterics lessened.

"We need to talk," Blade informed her when he felt she was capable of listening and understanding. "I have an offer to make."

"Offer?" Isabel repeated, blinking up at him and

dabbing at her moist eyes with her right hand. Her left, on her far side, moved back and forth as if rubbing the ground.

"How would you like to come live with us at our Home?" Blade inquired. "There are about one hundred men, women, and children there and they'd welcome you gladly."

Isabel stopped sniffling, a crafty gleam in her eyes. "They would, huh?"

"Yes. You could forget all about your past and start a new life."

"Liar."

"What?"

Sneering, Isabel pointed at the gunfighter. "You're a liar! I heard him talking. You plan to kill me."

Blade fixed a reproachful stare on Hickok.

At that instant, when the giant's attention was diverted, Isabel struck, whipping around the six-inch-long pointed piece of quartz that had been partially imbedded in the dirt until she tugged it loose with her left hand. She grinned as she swung, knowing the giant couldn't possibly evade her blow, relishing the thought of rupturing his throat. Her slender arm was an arrow, the quartz nearly to his neck, when the last sound she would ever hear fell on her ears.

A Colt Python revolver boomed once.

CHAPTER NINETEEN

As the twin Cy-Hounds bounded toward Yama he fired, sweeping the Dakon in a semicircle to catch both brutes full in the chest. The biochemical marvels reacted instantaneously, moving almost too fast for the human eye to follow, one darting to the left, the other the right, lowering their squat bodies to the floor as they ran. The rounds passed over their rushing forms without so much as nicking their skin.

The four scientists were less fortunate. Standing as they were directly behind the Cy-Hounds and lacking their creations' reflexes, the quartet took the brunt of the fragmentation bullets head-on. They were all hurled backwards, their torsos exploding, spraying gore all over the floor. Two of the men screamed horribly as they went down.

Seated in the chair, the Minister never exhibited a hint of emotion as the men died. He simply sat and watched the tableau unfold.

Yama swung to the left, tracking the one Cy-Hound,

his shots ripping up the floor just behind it as it ran in a tight loop. Fleetingly engrossed in nailing the beast, he failed to stay aware of the second, and realized the gravity of his mistake a millisecond later when the equivalent of a convoy truck doing 60 miles an hour hit him squarely between the shoulder blades.

Knocked forward over eight feet by the impact, Yama crashed onto his elbows and knees, losing his grip on the Dakon II. The rifle skidded off to the left.

Behind him the Minister vented a sinister laugh.

The Cy-Hound executing the loop abruptly changed direction and came straight for the Warrior.

Yama barely rose to his knees and the dog was there, slamming into him, bearing both of them to the carpet. He wedged his left forearm under the beast's mouth as they went down, preventing it from ripping his face off, and rolled to the right, striving to prevent it from gaining a purchase. Its claws tore into his body, causing intense pain that he ignored.

The second canine came to its fellow construct's aid, dashing in close and nipping at the big man's legs.

Still rolling, Yama grimaced at the agony, his right hand dropping to the survival knife and whipping the blade clear. He drove it up and in, sinking the gleaming tip deep into the Cy-Hound's left eye, burying the knife in the socket.

As if jolted by fifty thousand volts of electricity, the brute arched its spine and furiously tore away from the Warrior, scrambling several feet to the right and halting while shaking its head and appearing dazed.

The other Cy-Hound pounced.

Yama had his palms on the floor, about to shove upright, when the beast used its head as a battering ram and sent him flying rearward. He crashed into a chair, jarring his left shoulder, wincing in torment. Lunging to his feet, disoriented and bleeding from a dozen deep cuts, he tried to draw the Browning.

Again the other brute bore down, this time going for the big man's left leg and sinking its teeth into his thigh. Its jaws locked on and held fast.

Tottering to the left, Yama rained a flurry of punches on the Cy-Hound's head but couldn't dislodge it. He went for the Browning, and detected movement to his right before he could clear leather. Belatedly he saw his second bestial adversary leaping at his throat, and threw his right arm up to ward off the canine's fangs.

Even with the survival knife jutting from its ravaged socket, the Cy-Hound fought on. Out of the air it hurtled to bury its teeth in the Warrior's arm.

Now Yama had a dog on his leg and one on his arm. They were working in concert, using their combined weight and savage might in an effort to pull him down where they could finish him off in seconds. Blood coursed from his forearm and thigh, streaking their lips and jaws red.

"A commendable try, Warrior," the Minister said. "But you were doomed from the start. Technic superiority will prevail every time."

Yama felt himself weakening. The Cy-Hound on his right arm ground its teeth onto his bone, and waves of sheer anguish racked his brain. He was losing! In moments he would be dead!

So what?

The thought shocked him, made him pause despite the shaking and tearing of the brutes clinging to his flesh. So what if he died? Hadn't he learned that death was merely the rite of passage from one level of reality to another? Hadn't he learned to embrace death as the inevitable end of earthly life and the beginning of eternity? Why was he letting his innate instinct for survival supplant his hard-earned wisdom?

How soon we forget!

To the Minister, viewing the struggle with concealed glee, certain of the Warrior's demise, came a rude shock when he saw the man wearing the skull abruptly straighten and square those broad shoulders, those blue eyes suddenly blazing with an inner fire and steely resolve. He recoiled in his chair, stupefied.

Yama disregarded both Cy-Hounds, disregarded the loss of blood and the ragged tears in his limbs and body. He simply reached for the scimitar, hauling the brute attached to his right arm along, and grasped the familiar hilt. Then he planted his legs and refused to be budged an inch.

Marveling at the big man's resistance, the Minister glanced at the front door to his office as shooting erupted outside. When he looked back at the Warrior, he was stunned to see him lifting the injured Cy-Hound off the floor *with one arm*.

Yama raised his right forearm level with his face and locked his eyes on the one good orb of the Cy-Hound. He reached over with his left hand, grabbed the survival knife, and twisted.

The brute let go and fell to the floor.

Bunching his shoulder muscles, Yama swung the scimitar in a downward stroke aimed at the artificial canine chewing on his thigh. The curved blade cleaved its spine behind the front shoulders and sank a good six inches into its body. Immediately the creature released its grip and fell, its rear legs no longer able to receive mental impulses from the computer chip in its cranium.

Yama took a step backward, lifted the scimitar on high, and swung again, this time going for the nape of the beast's neck. In a glittering blur of light the blade severed its head from its body.

Gasping, the Minister rose, his hand to his throat.

The remaining Cy-Hound swung sideways to keep its intact eye on the Warrior. Coiling its legs, the brute twisted and vaulted at the human's neck.

With a speed that made lightning seem slow by comparison, Yama employed the scimitar as only a master swordsman could hope to do. In a single immensely powerful stroke he decapitated the dog, and heard both the head and body plop to the floor. Then, rotating slowly, he faced the ruler of Technic City.

His eyes widening, the Minister retreated a step and extended his left hand. "Wait! Don't do anything rash!"

Yama took a stride forward, his hands wrapped around the scimitar's hilt, the blade angled toward the carpet. His adamantine visage, ripped uniform, and blood-splattered form lent him the aspect of Death Incarnate.

The Minister looked and recognized his own demise in the Warrior's flaming eyes. He backpedaled a yard and cried, "You wanted to take me prisoner!"

"I've changed my mind," Yama said, the words a guttural growl, as he kept advancing.

There were yells from beyond the door to the reception area, and suddenly it burst open. In ran Ramis, his expression haggard, to halt in amazement at the carnage before him. "Excellency!" he wailed. "The rebels are here!"

The Minister paused, his eyes on the apparition stalking him. He considered trying to dart past the Warrior to escape, but realized he didn't stand a prayer. There was always the rear door to the stairwell, however. "Where are my guards?"

"All dead, sir," Ramis replied. "What do you want me to do?"

"Get help, fool!"

"Yes—" Ramis began, and ended his sentence in a strangled scream as a bullet from the doorway penetrated his head and felled him where he stood.

Yama ignored the shot. He moved inexorably nearer to the Minister, taking one slow stride after another. Ten feet separated them.

Into the chamber poured a dozen rebels. In their forefront was Falcone. He stopped, flabbergasted, but recovered quickly. "Yama! Don't!"

The Warrior halted and glanced at the leader of the Resistance.

"Don't kill him," Falcone stated. "We need him. We must put him on trial for all the people to see."

Through the stairwell door pounded a mix of rebels and citizens. They checked their rush in bewilderment.

"Please!" Falcone said earnestly, alarmed by the Warrior's countenance. It sent a chill down his spine. "We can use the Minister for propaganda purposes. Once we publicly dispose of him, the old Technic order will be permanently eradicated."

The Minister stiffened indignantly. "I'll never consent to letting common rabble put *me* on trial!" He walked toward the man who seemed to be the rebel leader, the same one he'd seen on television earlier.

Yama hadn't moved.

Falcone glared at the tyrant. "You don't have a say in the matter. A citizens' court will be convened and you'll be duly tried for your heinous crimes. We'll expose all the atrocities you've committed, all those perpetrated by the Technic system since the government was inaugurated, so all the people will know beyond a shadow of a doubt, so they'll never forget the price of letting freedom slip away."

Stopping, the Minister jabbed a bony finger at the rebel.

"Ignorant scum! What gives you the right to set yourselves up as my judge? You're beneath my contempt. I demand that you treat me with the respect I deserve."

Yama's grip on the scimitar tightened. "If that's what you want," he said softly but firmly, the statement carrying to every corner of the room.

The Minister glanced at him and smirked. "You're too late, Warrior. The war is over."

"Their war, maybe," Yama said, nodding at the rebels. "Not mine." He took a pace toward the ruler.

Aware of the implication, the Minister nervously looked at Falcone. "Who's in charge here, anyway?"

Yama took another step.

None of the rebels or citizens intervened. They were transfixed, intimidated by the Warrior and unwilling to incur his wrath, collectively certain that protest would prove futile.

Licking his lips, the Minister faced the big man and took a step rearward. "Why? Tell me why?"

"You already know."

"For her?"

The Warrior nodded once.

"But this is insane! I wasn't even the Minister at the time."

Yama stood a yard away. He waited, his gaze boring into the Minister, his body poised, knowing the man would break at any moment. Then he saw rampant fear flare in the tyrant's eyes, and the man attempted to run. "For Alicia," he said under his breath as he whipped the scimitar in a broad stroke.

Everyone in the chamber watched in perverse fascination as that glistening blade sliced the Minister's neck neatly in half and the blond head sailed through the air trailing a crimson spray. It thumped onto the floor and bounced twice before rolling to a stop at Falcone's feet.

"For Alicia," Yama repeated, louder, his voice choked with emotion.

No one bothered to ask what he meant.

One week later.

Yama stood at a window in the newly named Executive Office, staring wistfully out over the drastically changed metropolis, his hands clasped behind his back. The sidewalks were packed with happy throngs, among them members of the newly organized Citizens Militia who now served as the combined police force and military, the men and women who had enlisted proudly wearing their distinctive dark blue uniforms bearing ebony skulls on the backs.

His own uniform had been repaired by the grateful rebels. His body bore a score of bandages, and was sore but mending. Yet his soul was still in turmoil. He knew they'd arrived. How, he couldn't say. But the night before, as he'd spent another sleepless eight hours in the apartment the rebels had graciously allotted him, he'd sensed their presence.

At the mahogony desk sat Falcone, working feverishly signing papers, answering phones, and conversing with a constant stream of humanity who all had business with the just-installed President of New Chicago. In the week since the revolution, elections had been held and a fresh name bestowed on the city to signify the rebirth of liberty and the triumph of the people.

Roy suddenly entered and dashed up to the desk. "There are three strangers here to see you, Falcone," he reported anxiously.

"Outsiders?"

"Yes. They showed up at the west gate an hour ago. It appears they were all set to destroy the guard tower when they noticed the new blue uniforms on the guards and decided to talk instead of ambushing them," Roy detailed, his excitement obvious. He glanced at Yama and lowered his voice. "They're *Warriors.*"

Falcone straightened. "What? Show them right in."

"We're already here, Chuckles," declared one of three men coming through the doorway.

Falcone stared at them in surprise, instantly recognizing the buckskin-clad form of Hickok from the stories he'd heard. The other two, though, a giant and an Indian, were unknown to him although he wondered if the giant might be the legendary Blade. He smiled and stood. "I'm glad to meet you."

Strangely, the trio paid no attention to him. Instead, they walked over and halted behind Yama, who hadn't turned around although he had to know they were there.

The giant spoke in a quiet, almost gentle voice. "Time to go back and face the music, old friend."

CHAPTER TWENTY

The lower level of the immense reinforced concrete bunker known as B Block was filled to overflowing for the Warrior Review Board hearing. Every Family member wanted to attend, and except for the three Warriors comprising Omega Triad who were on guard duty on the ramparts of the high brick walls surrounding the 30-acre compound, all were present. They sat in folding metal chairs, stood three deep along the walls, and packed the stairs leading to the upper level.

Blade sat in a chair at a small table situated between the rows of spectators and the long table at the head of the room where the three presiding Warriors would sit. Lots had been drawn to determine which three of the 18 would sit on the Review Board, and he hadn't drawn one of the short straws, which had turned out for the best.

He glanced to his left at Yama, who sat beside him in stony silence with his eyes fixed on the front wall. Frowning, he shifted and looked back at the crowd. Among those in the front row were his wife and son. He waved and smiled at Jenny and Gabe, then nodded at the Family Leader, Plato, who sat on Jenny's left.

Most of the front row had been filled by the ten remaining Warriors, and among them were Hickok and Geronimo. All the Warriors wore grim expressions. They were acutely aware of the gravity of the proceedings, particularly since one of their own stood accused of such a grave breech of discipline.

The hushed conversations taking place abruptly ended when the three presiding Warriors entered and moved toward the long table.

Blade studied them, glad he wasn't in their shoes.

In the lead walked the diminutive Warrior named Rikki-Tikki-Tavi, clad in black as usual, the long scabbard containing his cherished katana clutched in his left hand. His Oriental features were inscrutable as he took his seat in the center of the three chairs positioned behind the long table.

Sitting down on the right was the Warrior called Lynx, a hybrid endowed with the attributes of a feline. His appearance resembled his namesake's, from his small triangular ears to his slanted green eyes to his coat of short, grayish-brown fur. The cat-man wore just a gray loincloth.

On Rikki's left sat a female Warrior, Bertha, a lovely dusky woman sporting a full Afro. She had on fatigues and combat boots. Like Lynx, she had been admitted to the Family in recent years, having spent most of her life in the ravaged Twin Cities of St. Paul and Minneapolis before being rescued by Alpha Triad.

Rikki-Tikki-Tavi somberly surveyed the chamber, then lifted the gavel that had been placed at the center of the table and slammed it down. "This Review Board Hearing is now in session. Will the accused please rise?"

Yama stood mechanically.

"You stand accused of one of the gravest offenses ever committed by any Warrior. Desertion is punishable three ways according to the Warrior bylaws. You can be expelled from the Family, never to set foot in the Home again. You can be stripped of your rank and forever denied Warrior status. Or this tribunal can select whatever punishment fits the crime. Do you fully appreciate the seriousness of your offense?"

"I do," Yama said softly.

"And how do you plead?"

"Guilty as charged."

Rikki leaned back and regarded his peer intently. "Have you any justification to offer for your actions?"

"I do not."

Blade quickly stood and regarded the three judges. "If I may, I would like to point out that the bylaws give any Warrior accused of a misdeed the right to defend himself or herself at a Review Hearing."

"We know that," Rikki said. "But if Yama refuses to do so, we'll be forced to render summary judgment."

Stepping around the small table, Blade indicated the Warrior in blue. "Yama's entire future with the Family is in jeopardy here. In light of this grave situation, I formally ask that I be permitted to offer a defense in Yama's behalf."

Bertha propped her elbows on the long table and cocked her head. "This is sort of unusual, ain't it?"

"Yeah," Lynx chimed in. "Why should we make an exception for this dummy?"

Blade controlled his temper and replied forcefully. "Because this is a man's future that's at stake. Because above all else judges are required to be fair and impartial. And because all of us are Warriors and pledged to do what is right at all times."

"I have no objections provided the accused agrees,"

Rikki announced, and looked at Yama. "Do you accept Blade's offer?"

"He asked me yesterday if he could defend me. Although I feel he is wasting his time, I won't stand in his way."

"Very well." Rikki turned to each of his fellow judges. "Do either of you object?"

Bertha and Lynx shook their heads.

"Very well," Rikki said, nodding at the giant. "You may proceed."

"Thank you," Blade said, trying to recall every word of the speech he had worked on until four in the morning. Once he'd realized that Yama intended to meekly accept whatever punishment was meted out, he'd decided to try this unorthodox tactic in an effort to save Yama from himself. "I won't attempt to dispute the facts. Yes, Yama departed the Home without authorization. Yes, he failed to show up for a scheduled shift. Had he left on his days off he would still be facing the same charges. He is, plain and simple, guilty."

A murmur broke out among the spectators.

Rikki banged the gavel and gave them a stern look. "Silence will be maintained at all times or the hearing will be conducted in private." He paused, focused on Blade. "Continue."

"Since the facts are indisputable I would like to call attention to the extenuating circumstances leading up to Yama's desertion and the consquences of his act," Blade said. "We all know about Alicia Farrow. We can all imagine what Yama went through. But can we also imagine the hell he has endured during the two years since her death?"

The three judges listened attentively.

"If you've ever known what it's like to be in love—and I know all three of you do—then you can envision how you'd feel if your loved one was murdered in front of your eyes. And I'd be willing to bet that each and every one of you would go after the party responsible."

"You've got that right, Big Guy," Lynx commented. "I'd rip the sucker to shreds."

Polite laughter rippled among the crowd.

Blade gestured at Yama. "Exactly. So think about the torment he endured. For two years he denied himself an outlet for his feelings. He bottled them up inside. And we all know what happens when a person does that. They build and build until they finally explode." He frowned. "Recently Yama, Samson, and I fought a Technic contingent in Green Bay. I believe that experience triggered Yama's long-suppressed urge to retaliate for Alicia's death. He could no longer control those feelings long denied. Although he knew it was wrong, he couldn't resist the impulse to go after the Technics."

"Why didn't he just ask permission to take off?" Bertha interrupted.

"Because he knew such permission would be denied," Blade replied. "Had it been, he probably would have stayed and continued to suffer as he had for years."

"His motivation is understandable," Rikki said, "but in itself does not justify his offense."

"True," Blade said. "But let's take a look at the consequences of his action. You're all aware that the Technics have been overthrown. New Chicago has become a democracy and plans to apply for membership in the Freedom Federation." He shifted so the spectators could also hear every word. "I was told by President Falcone, their new leader, that the revolution wouldn't have succeeded without Yama. He inspired them to launch it. He singlehandedly attacked the Central Core and disrupted the Technic Government. The people of Chicago hail him as a hero. And to give you an idea of how grateful they really are, their Militia has adopted a dark blue uniform with a black skull on the back.''

All eyes were fixed on the accused.

"In light of Yama's motivation and the fact that one of the Family's worst enemies has been defeated because of his dereliction of duty, I plead for leniency,'' Blade went on. "I ask you to put yourself in his shoes and temper your judgment with mercy.''

Rikki-Tikki-Tavi looked at Yama. "Have you anything further to add?''

"Just that I will wholeheartedly accept whatever punishment you see fit to hand down,'' Yama said. "I know I've done wrong. Not that it matters, but the shame is almost unbearable.''

"Your comments will be taken into consideration,'' Rikki said, and scanned the chamber. "This Review Board will be in recess for an hour while a judgment is reached.'' He used the gavel again, rose, and led Bertha and Lynx from the room.

Everyone began talking at once.

Yama turned to Blade. "I'm grateful for your help.''

"What are friends for?''

"I'm sorry for all the trouble I've caused you.''

Blade shrugged. "We do what we have to.''

The afternoon sun had warmed the temperature to 65 degrees. Yama stood under a tree not far from B Block and watched a cloud shaped like a turtle sail to the southeast. The fresh air felt good.

"Yama?''

He turned and saw her standing a few feet off, as beautiful as ever in a faded pink blouse and patched jeans. Her dark brown hair hung to her shoulders. Anxiety was mirrored in her green eyes.

"Mind if we talk?''

"Not at all, Melissa," Blade said. "I still have half an hour before the Review Board is back in session."

She came closer, her hands clasped tightly at her waist. "What do you think they'll decide?"

"There's no telling."

"Rikki is one of your best friends. Surely he wouldn't agree to expelling you."

Yama gazed at the departing turtle. "Rikki is first and foremost a Warrior, one of the best the Family has ever had. He'll go by the book in whatever he decides."

"It hardly seems fair," Melissa commented, moving to the tree and leaning against the trunk.

"You're new to the Family. Once you've lived here a while you'll understand."

A tense silence ensued.

"May I ask you a question?" Melissa said after a bit.

"Anything."

"What happens between us now?"

"Us?" Yama repeated, looking at her.

"You know what I mean," Melissa stated, sounding hurt. "You know how I feel about you, how I've felt ever since you showed up in Green Bay and saved me from the Automatons. And I thought you felt the same way about me."

"I do," Yama confirmed.

"Then how could you go off without saying good-bye, without even letting me know what you were up to?"

"You would have tried to stop me."

"Damn straight."

"So I believed it best to simply leave," Yama said, and sighed. "It was one of the hardest things I've ever done."

Melissa studied his face. "And have you laid the ghosts to rest?"

"Yes," Yama answered confidently. "At long, long last I've settled accounts with my past. I don't have the weight of Alicia Farrow's death on my shoulders any more.''

"Thank God," Melissa said, and beamed.

"Why are you so happy?''

"Because I don't have to compete with a ghost any longer. Now maybe you'll loosen up and let our relationship develop.''

Yama reached out and tenderly touched her cheek. "I'd like that,'' he stated, then frowned. "But we shouldn't be talking like this with my future hanging in the balance. We'll wait and hear the verdict.''

"What difference does it make?'' Melissa asked. "If you're expelled, I'm going with you.''

The Warrior did a double take. "You are not.''

"You can't stop me.''

"But you're safer here. You know the conditions prevailing in the Outlands. A couple by themselves would be fair game for every raider, scavenger, mutation, and wild beast out there.''

"I'd rather be with you no matter where you are. The reason I came to the Home was to be with you. If you leave, I don't want to stay.''

Shaking his head, Yama stared at B Block. "I refuse to take you along.''

"Then I'll go by myself.''

"You wouldn't.''

"Try me.''

They locked eyes, hers moist and appealing, his hard but melting. Uttering a sharp cry, she ran into his arms and hugged him close, pressing her face to his neck.

"I don't want to lose you.''

Yama stroked her hair, feeling her tears on his skin, and his entire body trembled.

"Are you all right?'' she whispered.

"Fine,'' he said, the word a haunted growl.

* * *

Again the lower chamber was packed. Anxious expectation hung thick and heavy over the spectators as they
observed the Review Board judges returning to the long
table.

"Will the accused please rise," Rikki-Rikki-Tavi stated.

The Warrior in blue slowly stood.

So did Blade. He glanced at his friend, saw the torment
reflected in Yama's countenance, and hoped for the best.

Rikki cleared his throat. "After due deliberation this
tribunal has reached a verdict. The decision is unanimous.
Considering the nature of the offense, an equal punishment is called for."

Blade swallowed, noting the severe expressions on all
three members of the Board. He realized he'd failed, and
dreaded the words he was about to hear.

"Before I pronounce sentence, an explanation is called
for," Rikki said, addressing the assembled Family. "This
is an exceptional case. True, twice before Warriors have
gone over the wall, so to speak, yet the circumstances
behind their departures were somewhat different. We
can't use the judgments rendered in their cases as
precedents for this one."

Every person present hung on Rikki's statements.

"Given the three options we had in deciding this case,
we chose the most appropriate. None of us wanted to strip
Yama of his Warrior status and have him live on at the
Home as a Tiller or Carpenter. Not that there is any stigma
attached to these vocations. Far from it. All classes at the
Home are equal. But in effect we would be condemning
Yama to a lifetime of personal humiliation," Rikki said.
"We've decided to make the punishment immediate and
effective."

For a moment Blade's hopes soared. If they weren't

willing to boot Yama from the Warrior ranks, perhaps they would go easy on him.

Rikki straightened and stared at the accused. "Yama, for your desertion and dereliction of duty, it is the judgment of this Review Board that you be expelled from the Family."

A collective intake of breath came from the spectators. Several Warriors bowed their heads.

Blade heard a plaintive wail, and looked back to see Melissa with her face buried in her arms, sobbing quietly. He turned to Yama, who resembled a statue, his heart going out to the man.

"However," Rikki continued, "because of the extenuating circumstances, and because of the invaluable assistance Yama gave to the Resistance Movement in New Chicago, our punishment will be suspended for one year. During that time Yama will be on strict probation. If he commits no further violations, at the end of the year all charges will be dropped, his slate will be wiped clean, and he will be free to live out the rest of his days at the Home."

The drop of a pin could have been heard, and then the Family erupted in a tremendous uproar of cheers and whoops of joy. Warriors laughed and patted each other on the back. There were tears in many an eye.

Blade went to shake Yama's hand, to offer his congratulations, but someone got there ahead of him.

A streak of pink and blue dashed up to the man wearing the skull and threw herself into his arms. They embraced, Melissa flushed with joy. Yama glanced at Blade and mouthed a silent "Thank you." Then he pressed his lips to hers.

Smiling, Blade walked to his family and hugged his wife.

Gabe tugged on his father's pants. ''Yama was pretty lucky, wasn't he?''

"I'd say he's very lucky," Blade responded.

"He looks real happy."

"Right now he's the happiest man alive."